CLUES TO THE EX
FOUR-TIME EDGAR
ROBERT BARNARD

"Having started out at a high level of ingenuity and humor, Barnard gets better, novel by novel. . . . Rich with character and . . . atmosphere . . . wickedly witty."
—*The Washington Post*

"You can count on a Barnard mystery being witty, intelligent, and a joy to read."
—*Publishers Weekly*

"The reigning master of English mystery/comedy. . . . Another of the author's unfailingly entertaining forays into crime."
—*Kirkus Reviews*

"One of England's most skillful and sardonic writers."
—*St. Louis Post-Dispatch*

"Barnard [has] an eye for the self-delusion and hypocrisy in all of us . . . and the result is a growing series of mysteries that are entertaining, often quite funny . . . and acutely observing."
—*The Boston Globe*

"There is no one quite like Barnard in his ability to combine chills and chuckles and to sprinkle the whole with delicious irony."
—*The San Diego Union*

BOOKS BY ROBERT BARNARD

THE
Case
OF THE
Missing
Brontë

●————————

Robert Barnard

A DELL BOOK

Published by
Dell Publishing
a division of
Bantam Doubleday Dell Publishing Group, Inc.
666 Fifth Avenue
New York, New York 10103

ISBN: 0-440-11108-0

Reprinted by arrangement with Charles Scribner's Sons

Printed in the United States of America

Published simultaneously in Canada

Two previous Dell editions

New Dell edition

May 1989

10 9 8 7 6 5 4 3 2 1

KRI

CONTENTS

THE
Case
OF THE
Missing
Brontë

CHAPTER 1

INTERRUPTED JOURNEY

'Can we stop and send a few postcards?' said Jan, as we drove through Hutton-le-Dales. 'I just love these small Yorkshire villages.'

'Heaven on a postcard, hell to live in,' I muttered.

'Oh, you're just grumpy,' said Jan.

And I suppose I was. Jan, Daniel, our son, and I had been spending an early summer holiday with what remains of my family in Northumberland. Seeing my sister again was all right, but she was so taken up with her baby that we might have been day trippers passing through for all the notice she took of us. For the rest there was my Aunt Sybilla, increasingly uncertain on her pins, who had taken to wearing monstrous turbans in the Edith Sitwell style — except that where Dame Edith carried hers off, Sybilla in hers looked as if she had been extinguished by some enormous candle-snuffer. Then there was my hygienic cousin Mordred, who has taken over the running of the house as a showplace, and is now the complete æsthete's tour-guide, full of out-of-the-way information and one-up jokes. And my Aunt Kate, much occupied with the fortunes of some ultra-rightist paramilitary splinter group of the National Front, whose slogan is 'Keep England Anglo-Saxon.' No, it wasn't much of a summer holiday. Broadmoor would have been more restful. I probably was grumpy.

I was even grumpier after we had stopped for twenty minutes for Jan to write postcards and Daniel to eat something fluorescent on a stick, because we no sooner got started again than, two minutes outside Hutton-le-

Dales, the car belched, coughed wheezily, and chugged to a halt. I blamed Jan, of course. I'm a great believer in the idea that if you keep going in an old car, things will probably be all right: stopping only gives it the chance to meditate on what's wrong with itself. Anyway, I poked around experimentally in the engine, and could find nothing amiss. It seemed to have an automobile version of one of those nervous diseases that kept Victorian women chained to their sofas. So we trudged back to the garage on the road out of Hutton, and the proprietor fetched the car in and pronounced that he would need to get a part from Leeds. That I could have guessed. As it was now nearly five, he wouldn't be able to get it till the morning. That I could have guessed too. Bang went our chances of getting home that night.

'I'll have the old girl ready for you by midday t'morrow,' said the garage man, patting her bonnet as if she were indeed an ailing maiden lady. 'And I can't say fairer than that, can I?'

I thought that if he had been willing to get his finger out, he could have said a lot fairer than that. But garage men — like plumbers and electricians — are part of the modern aristocracy, people one insults at one's peril. I sighed, and asked if the local pub took overnight guests.

'Well, they do, as a rule, like, but Mrs Martin — that's t'landlord's missis — has been poorly, and I doubt they'd be willing. There's Mrs Hebden down the road: she does bed and breakfast in the season. Happen she'll take you. Why don't you try?'

There seemed to be no option but to throw ourselves on the mercies of Mrs Hebden, so we shoved a few necessaries into a bag and traipsed off in the direction pointed out to us. She lived in a sturdy, grey-stone Edwardian house, three stories high, at the other end of the village. When she first opened the door, she looked suspiciously at us in the gaunt, bony way some Yorkshire women have, but it was really only the local wariness, and as she told us later she had been 'that plagued with Jehovah's Witnesses of late' that it was not surprising. When we had explained to her what we wanted, she became half-way gracious.

'Well, I could, I suppose,' she said. 'If it would suit. It's nothing grand.'

It was two clean bedrooms, with the offer of baths, and a high tea at only £1.50 extra a head. It seemed grand enough to us. We trooped in, and gradually we took over the house, as always happens when there is a child around. Over tea Daniel regaled Mrs Hebden (whose gauntness turned out to be a matter of bone rather than spirit) with descriptions of my Aunt Sybilla — descriptions which made her sound like something out of the Brothers Grimm. We decided he must have scored a decided hit, because after we had made a splendid meal, Mrs Hebden volunteered to baby-sit if we would like to go to the pub for a drink.

'Oh yes, *please* go,' said Daniel. 'Then I can tell her about Aunt Kate.'

So, not at all reluctant, that is what we did. We walked through the village, which was basically the one street of sandstone houses and cottages, with other cottages set back down side lanes, and after a bit of a walk around the countryside we settled into the pub, the Dalesman, for a quiet beer. After a week of my Aunt Kate's dandelion wine (which seemed to have curdled rather than matured) not even champagne could have cheered us up better. The reputation of Yorkshire village pubs is that you have to drink regularly there for a year before they so much as nod good-evening to you. But like so much people say about Yorkshire, this turned out not to be true, or not true of this pub. Bill Martin, the landlord, was a foreigner himself, coming from close to the Yorkshire-Lancashire border, so he was broad-minded enough to welcome a pair who, coming from London, could almost be classed as Undesirable Immigrants. The other drinkers were mostly old men, and though they didn't volunteer any observations, or expect anything from us, they smiled cheerily enough. I was disappointed: they ought to have been looking at us with hell-fire in their glances.

So we were all set for a nice cosy evening. Jan and I settled into a corner, and began to have our first real talk for a week. As usual with horrific occasions, this one began to seem almost jolly in retrospect (did the Sabine women, I wonder, get together in old age to giggle over former times?). I told Jan of my interview with Aunt Sybilla, closeted alone, during which she had complained bitterly about what she termed my refusal to take over the headship of the family.

'The headship of the family was never really on offer,' I had protested.

'You could have had it if you had *fought*,' she had said, 'fought for it in the true tradition of the Trethowan family. Or made Wally an offer.'

'Making an offer is much more in the tradition of this family than fighting,' I had said, and she had glared — malevolent little eyes peeping out from under twenty folds of turban. For Aunt Sybilla has constructed an imaginary line of crusader knights and Tudor magnates for us, which has quite eclipsed in her mind the reality of hard-fisted mill-owners, borne aloft on wings of brass.

Jan in her turn told me of her session exchanging recipes with Aunt Kate, the experimental gastronome of the family. When she was offered an exclusive recipe from the sweets chef at the Savoy (whose wife Jan went to school with); a recipe involving three days' soaking, marinading, slow-boiling, and God knows what else, she had read the thing through, put it aside, and said: 'These restaurant chefs are so unin*vent*ive, aren't they?'

Anyway, we were rolling around about this and some of the other eccentricities of my appalling family, when the pub door opened, and a little old lady came in. Well, not really little—and in fact not all that old: about five feet eight and sixty-three, if you want my guess. But there was something slightly old-fashioned and spinsterish about her, something un-with-it, that invited the description. Her clothes were smart enough, but in a fashion of several years ago—rather severe, with the skirt down to the calves, though the frilliness of the blouse somewhat mitigated the formality. Her hair was grey, her eyes keen but friendly, and she clutched a capacious blue leather handbag.

'Good evening, Bill,' she greeted the landlord. 'The usual, please. Good evening, Harry . . . Joseph . . . Bert.'

She got friendly nods from all the locals. She was obviously a regular in the sort of pub where normally a woman on her own would be nervous about intruding. However, when she had got her drink, a gin and tonic, and paid for it, she went to sit with none of the locals, but brought it over to our corner, and brightly said:

'Do you mind if I join you?'

It's an unanswerable question at the best of times, and though we were in fact enjoying at last being on our own again, we jumped up, cleared a space for her, and muttered our names.

'I'm Edith Wing,' she announced. 'I live here—the cottage up Carter's Lane, if you know it. Oh, but of course—you wouldn't. You must be visitors, of course. Are you the first of our holiday-makers?'

'Not really,' I said. 'It's more involuntary. Our car broke down.'

'Oh, of course. I should have connected. I saw a strange Morris 1100 sitting in the garage forecourt. One notices things like that in a place this size. How fortunate. For us, I mean. We don't get so many visitors, even in the summer, that we can afford to waste them.'

'You make us sound like precious metal,' Jan said.

'Well, of course, you are—to me. It's a lovely life here . . . so peaceful . . . but one does miss, just a little, the contact with the outside world . . . the stimulus. I used to be a schoolmistress, you see. *Quite* a good school. Broadlands. Further to the north of the county. We used to pride ourselves on being open and receptive—not too fuddy-duddy. And we had a great number of distinguished old girls, who brought in a breath of the outside world when they returned for visits. I retired early, and I do sometimes miss that. I've seen so many mistresses, colleagues, you know, retire and go—well, funny, to put the matter bluntly. I wouldn't like the same to happen to me.'

'I do know what you mean,' I said. 'When they haven't got a job to do every day, they sort of go off. It's not just schoolmistresses that happens to. I've known policemen go the same way.'

'I'm sure. So you're a policeman? Fascinating. In London? How wonderful. The centre of crime, as it were. I've always longed to be in the centre, but I've always had to be satisfied with the periphery. And do you work, my dear?'

'Arabic—I study Arabic,' said Jan. 'I've just finished.'

'How clever of you to pick a coming subject. It must *be* a coming subject, mustn't it? I'm afraid my subjects were geography and biology, and however much one tried to make them interesting to the girls, one always had the slight suspicion that there was something *musty* about them, goodness knows why.'

She settled herself well down into her chair, and took a parsimonious sip of her gin.

'These last few weeks I've been wishing my subjects had been history, or English, or something that could be really useful to me at the moment.'

She seemed to be one of those direct, forthright souls who ignore the usual middle-class discretions and confide their business to the world whether the world wants it or not. Because it only needed Jan to say 'Oh?' for her to launch straight into her current preoccupation.

'It was my cousin, you see, Rose Carbury, who died in February. She was a schoolmistress too—deputy head of a very nice little private school in Scarborough. We were distant cousins, but we were friends as well, and we used to meet when we could. Now and then we'd have a weekend in London—for a play, and the museums. We were typical schoolteachers, as you can see. Now, Rose retired last year, and she was already sick, poor thing. She had a cottage the other side of Leeds, and I went up there as often as I could, stayed with her, tried to cheer her up. There were nearer relatives in the area, but they—well, let's just say that they weren't close. So when she died, Rose left all the family valuables to this nephew and niece—she thought that was only right—but she left her library (so valuable to someone in retirement) and all her papers to me. Much of it was old stuff that she'd had packed away in her attic.'

'I love old papers,' said Jan.

'Yes, indeed. This was mostly family stuff: letters and wills and so on. And of course it is my family as well. But that's why I've felt the need for a historian's training—to know what is valuable and what isn't. It cost a mint of money to get the stuff here, I can tell you, and I don't want to throw out anything that might be useful or valuable. It's been fascinating going through it, as you can imagine.'

'I'm sure it has,' said Jan. 'You should take care of it all, if you have the space. Libraries are keen on that kind of stuff for their archives.'

'Of course they are. And I'm sure that's what Rose would have wanted. The family, you know, made a fuss about my having it, but . . . well, they're funny people. But the fact is that now I've come upon something that's quite different.'

She said it with a queer air of excitement, and she snapped open her handbag and took from it, enclosed in a folder, a yellowing sheet of paper. It was a large sheet, folded twice, and cut roughly along the edges. Each of the small pages thus produced was covered from top to bottom with tiny writing — almost a child's writing, for each letter was separate from the other. But no child could have written such a tiny script, one would have thought. And when I looked closely I found that new paragraphs were marked off with a stroke, and there were frequent speech marks. This was certainly no child's essay.

'It looks like part of a story of some kind,' I said. Jan took it and pored over it, but kept silent.

'It does, doesn't it?' said Miss Edith Wing. 'But I think it must be more than that. Because there are pages and pages of it — at least two hundred, I should say, and probably more.'

'A novel,' I said. And then it struck me, and I looked at Jan. 'But — that handwriting . . .'

'You are slow, Perry,' said Jan. 'And you're supposed to be so literary. It's *just* like the Brontës. Like those little poems and diaries we saw at Haworth last year.'

. 'And those childish booklets,' said Miss Wing. 'You know, that's what I've been thinking. Naturally I've been to Haworth now and then, with the girls. But I feel so foolish, so unqualified. Of course I've read *Jane Eyre* and the other things, but *so* many years ago!'

I took the page back; and tried to decipher it.

'I don't recognize it,' I said. 'But then, I wouldn't necessarily. But these names here — Thomas Blackmore, Marian Thornley . . . Lingdale Manor. I don't remember any of them.'

'Neither do I,' said Jan. I refrained from pointing out that this was probably due to the fact that she had not read any of the Brontë novels.

'I feel so uncertain,' said Edith Wing. 'It could be anything, couldn't it? Perhaps lots of people had handwriting like that in those days. Awfully paper-saving it must have been. On the other hand, it could be an early draft of one of the Brontë novels. Or even an unpublished one—'

'Another novel by Emily Brontë!' I said.

'Because you see, long, long ago our family did have some connections with them. Not with Emily, though. With Anne and Branwell. Mrs Robinson, who employed them as governess and tutor to her children, was my five-times great-grandmother. Or is it six? Anyway, it's not something we usually tell people about, because there was a scandal at the time . . .'

'I remember,' I said. 'She seduced Branwell, or he seduced her, or something.'

'We don't admit that in the family,' said Miss Wing, primly. 'But it's what most people thought. So you see—there *is* a connection.'

'How absolutely extraordinary,' I said.

'What are you going to do?' asked Jan.

'That's what I wondered,' said Miss Wing, looking very perplexed. 'Of course, it could be some kind of forgery . . .'

'Then why keep it secret all these years?' I said. 'All that effort, just to hide it away? That's more unbelievable than the idea that it could be a genuine Brontë novel. Forgeries are made to be sold, believe me. Obviously you are going to have to get in touch with an expert. I think the best thing to do would be to take it to Haworth.'

'I thought of that,' said Edith Wing. 'But it's more than forty miles away, and such a difficult place to get to, if like me you have no car. First to Leeds, then the train to

Keighley, then bus. And that hill! Perhaps later in the summer I could manage it.'

'I really shouldn't leave something like that lying around in your cottage. Isn't Milltown fairly near here?'

'About thirteen miles.'

'Well, they've got one of those newish universities there, haven't they? There's bound to be someone or other there who would know something about it. If I were you I'd get in contact with them.'

The awful thing is, that with those words I very nearly sent her to her death.

CHAPTER 2

THE BRONTË BUG

The next week, as you can imagine, was devoted to Brontë research. We had been left, after all, on a knife edge. On the journey back to London Jan talked about practically nothing else, and as soon as we got into the flat she took down *Wuthering Heights* and stayed up half the night with it. The next day we went to the local library and fetched home a formidable pile of books.

I suppose you thought, when I said in the last chapter that Jan had never read anything by the Brontës, that this was just a piece of husbandly snide. Actually it is quite true. Jan went to one of those schools built in London in the late 'fifties: plate glass, unlimited equipment, variable teaching and a surfeit of new ideas. In Jan's school any books they read had to be 'relevant' (by implication 'to the contemporary situation'), and since she was at school in the late 'sixties, you can imagine what that meant. She has read lots of Brecht, novels by David Storey and Sillitoe, and she's performed in plays by

Edward Bond and such like. I have this reactionary notion that one can be educated without any knowledge of the works of Edward Bond, but not without any knowledge of the works of Emily Brontë. Anyway, except for a dreadful film from some years back in which all the characters seemed to be epileptics (an odd idea — it wasn't even the year of the handicapped), Jan had had no contact with *Wuthering Heights*. Naturally it bowled her over.

Poring over the various books from the library, we came quite early to the conclusion that the handwriting on the page we saw most resembled Emily's — for example, her handwriting in those oddly childish diary fragments she and Anne wrote. Probably Emily had other handwritings too: Charlotte had a flowing script for the fair copies of her novels — quite rightly, because no publisher even then would have consented to read the tiny script she had used for the childhood booklets. Presumably Emily had the same. But this was her private script — for drafts, poems, personal things.

Then we got down to the biographies. These, especially in the case of Emily and Anne, were really quite odd, as practically nothing is known of them, and the books were exercises in strawless brick-making. Some pretty peculiar bricks they came up with, too. All sorts of things, to change the metaphor, which would not have stood up for a moment in a court of law. The odd thing was, too, that for quite long periods the biographers didn't really know where Emily and Anne were — at school, governessing, or at Haworth? Though Charlotte conducted regular and frequent exchanges of letters with her friends, she hardly ever mentioned them. No doubt she was too wrapped up in her own adolescent emotional and spiritual crises. Until 1845, when they all gathered at the Parsonage after the débâcle of Branwell's affair with Mrs Robinson, there are great gaps in our knowledge of their lives.

After that, as the tragedy sped to its conclusion, the biographies were full, and more securely based. But I was immediately struck with one thing. In 1845 the sisters began collecting together their poems, which were published in 1846. In 1846, too, *Wuthering Heights* was finished, to be published (after frustrating delays) in 1847. But from Spring 1846 to the time she died at the end of 1848, Emily wrote virtually nothing. She wrote a torrid narrative poem, and began revising it. As far as her literary life was concerned there was, according to all the biographers, a two and a half year blank.

The funny thing was, this didn't seem to worry those biographers at all. They had constructed in their minds a picture of a moody, lonely, recalcitrant genius — touchy, unapproachable, careless of literary success. You rather wondered that such a creature should ever care to send her work to a publisher in the first place. But, by their account, when the poems failed and *Wuthering Heights* was misunderstood, she simply withdrew into her shell and wrote no more.

A lot of this may have been true, of course, though precious little was the evidence they had for it, I must say. I was willing to believe that Emily was a difficult creature; not the sort of girl one would take along to the Annual Police Ball. What I was sceptical about was the 'careless of literary fame' line. I've known a few authors, mainly in my childhood, and one thing I know about them is that nary a one is careless of literary fame. And another thing I know is that as soon as a novelist has a novel accepted, he sits down and writes another one. It's a sort of nervous tic. No doubt the facts that the poems sold only four copies, and the publisher of *Wuthering Heights*, a Mr Newby, turned out to be a crook, were depressing. But how much literature would there be if everyone gave up writing because their publisher was crooked? I refused to believe that during those more than two years, until she fell ill in the autumn of 1848, Emily was for the first time in her adult life idle — idle, that is, in a literary sense.

'I know I'd be scribbling away like mad,' said Jan.

'You're hardly the Emily Brontë type,' I said. 'But yes — I bet she was too.'

Two more things struck us very forcibly. The first was that after Charlotte's death a note was found in Emily's desk, in an envelope addressed to Ellis Bell (her pseudonym). It was from Newby, her scamp publisher — but it was a perfectly sensible letter, expressing interest in a 'second work' which had clearly been mentioned to him, but advising her to take time and care, since second novels were a difficult hurdle. Here was first-rate, police-court evidence of a second novel. But what did the biographers do? Most of them assumed it was a letter to Anne about *The Tenant of Wildfell Hall*, and that it had somehow got pushed into the wrong envelope.

The second thing that struck me was the chaotic state of Brontë manuscripts. Charlotte's husband, at the end of a long life, and in what one can only take to have been a state of senility, let them fall into the hands of a rogue and a forger. This man, Thomas J. Wise, had played fast and loose with the manuscripts, to increase their value to avid British and American collectors. For example, he had taken them apart and had sewn up little bits of Charlotte's manuscripts (valuable) with great wadges of Branwell's manuscripts (not very valuable). Lots of important material had simply disappeared from sight. Only a few years before an American scholar had put together two manuscript fragments widely separated in two learned libraries and had come up with four chapters of what was apparently Charlotte Brontë's first attempt at a proper novel. Before then, those pieces had been virtually unknown. If Thomas J. Wise's reputation as a forger was rather discouraging, this story was a real pick-me-up, proving that even today discoveries were still waiting to be made.

As you can imagine, all this research took most of our spare time, and though Jan had a fair bit of this, having just finished her degree at Newcastle, and being in a state of suspended animation waiting for the results, still Daniel got mildly neglected all the next week. He proved his nice nature by reading a lot, running as wild as a boy can do in the streets of Maida Vale, and fixing a lot of his own food. Jan and I, meanwhile, were mulling over the whole thing incessantly.

'What I can't believe,' said Jan, 'is this notion that when she finished *Wuthering Heights*, and when it was accepted, she just sat around like a gawbie for well over two years. It's not as though Haworth offered an infinite variety of other occupations, seeing it was at that time the original back of beyond. As far as I can see she didn't even go to church. It was Charlotte who taught Sunday school and all that kind of thing. Emily had been writing for fifteen years, and then suddenly she stopped. I don't believe a word of it.'

'There was Branwell,' I said, forcing myself against the grain to fill the position of Devil's Advocate and damper of Jan's hopes. 'She seems to have been the only one to have any time for him.'

'Branwell must have been a trial, but he can hardly have been a full-time occupation. In those months Anne wrote another novel, Charlotte wrote most of *Jane Eyre* and half of *Shirley*—and Emily, nothing at all.'

'Well, I agree it's pretty odd. But it's a long way from saying that to saying that what Miss Wing has is it. Emily may have destroyed it herself. Charlotte may have, after her death.'

'Well, if so, what's this?'

'For a start,' I said, 'there's the forger.'

'Forgeries, as you rightly said to Miss Wing, are made

to be sold, not to be stored away, to turn up years later among the papers of a family with Brontë connections.'

'What about Miss Wing as a forger herself?'

'Honestly, did she look like one?'

'Not in the least. But then, I've known one or two forgers, and I'd be hard put to it to generalize about the type. Well, then, if it's not a forgery, perhaps it's an early novel by Charlotte. All the children's handwriting was very similar, that's why Thomas J. Wise got away with his dirty tricks with the manuscripts. Or it might be by Branwell. A novel by Branwell is a definite possibility. That would explain, too, how it could have lain there so long: it wouldn't have anything like as great a commercial value.'

'Branwell could never have written a novel,' objected Jan. 'He wasn't a stayer.'

'You only say that because the biographers say it. He stayed with the Robinsons at Blake Hall twice as long as Charlotte ever stayed at any of her governess jobs. If Mrs Robinson had been a bolter, perhaps Branwell would have been a stayer. After all, if Charlotte had died in 1845, exactly the same would have been said about her. She'd never stuck to anything.'

'Hmmm,' said Jan dubiously. 'It was always perfectly clear that there was more to Charlotte than there was to Branwell. He was the despair of the family, right from the time he grew up. And I can't see the love of Mrs Robinson making much difference to him. We don't even know that he ever *had* an affair with her. Daphne du Maurier thinks it was with one of the daughters.'

'I expect someone, somewhere, is writing a book to prove it was with the Robinson boy who was his pupil. Then we'll have covered all the possibilities.'

'Any more bright ideas about what the manuscript could be?'

'Let's see . . . I say, what if it turned out to be one of

those awful modern sequels—*Return to Wuthering Heights*, or something? There was a rash of them a few years ago. All they lacked was genius.'

'Written in Emily's tiny hand to give verisimilitude, I suppose? Come off it, Perry, you can do better than that. You know, this is unbearable. How do you think we'll hear? Is it the sort of thing that would get into the papers?'

'Oh, sure. If it were authenticated. But it'll take years before anyone gets to that point.'

'Oh, for God's sake, Perry, I can't wait *years*. I'm dying of the suspense as it is. Why can't we go back there and ask her? Or even give her a ring?'

'Really, Jan, you don't imagine I'd drive all that way on the off-chance . . .' But actually, when it came to the point, I thought I might be forced to that. So I continued rather feebly: 'Anyway, we obviously ought to try to ring up first. At the moment we don't even know she's gone to anyone at the University of Milltown.'

'Couldn't we try ringing her, Perry? After all, she did rather drag us into the whole thing, didn't she, so she can't blame us for wanting to follow it up.'

'We'll have to give her a bit *longer*, Jan. I mean, even if she has contacted an expert, she won't have got a snap judgment. You know what that sort is like. It could be months before they even give a highly tentative and preliminary judgment, hedged around with ifs and buts and "to the best of our knowledges".'

As luck would have it, it was at that moment that the telephone rang in the hall.

'Perry Trethowan,' I said.

'Perry Trethowan, you're a perpetual surprise to me,' said the voice of Assistant Commissioner Joe Grierley, my boss. 'I never knew you had Yorkshire connections, Perry.'

'Northumberland,' I corrected him. 'You know that

perfectly well.'

'Yorkshire,' insisted Joe. 'Here are people asking about you from Yorkshire. When were you there last?'

'We passed through last week, as a matter of fact.'

'Exactly. Leaving behind indelible memories, apparently. Why do people remember you, Perry? Is it your size?'

'It's because my father got done in in totally ridiculous circumstances and you insisted on sending me to help clear it up. What is all this, Joe? I'm off until six o'clock.'

'Did you meet an elderly lady in a pub? In a village called Hutton-le-Dales?'

'I did. We did. Jan and Daniel were with me.'

'So I gather. Will you speak to this bloke from Yorkshire? Something's come up, and he thought you could help.'

Naturally I assented, very much less grudgingly than would normally be the case during my off-duty time. We were not, obviously, to lose contact with Miss Edith Wing. I waited, while complicated things were done on the switchboard at Scotland Yard, and eventually I heard a gentle, tired Yorkshire voice.

'Superintendent Trethowan?'

'Yes.'

'I'm sorry to bother you off-duty. Has the Assistant Commissioner given you some idea what it's about?'

'Not really. But yes, my wife and I did talk to an old lady in a pub in Hutton-le-Dales. Edith Wing the name was.'

'Yes, exactly. I'm afraid you were recognized. Now, what did you talk about?'

'Oh, mainly about a manuscript she'd discovered among papers she'd inherited.'

'Do you know what this manuscript was?'

'No, at least, not anything definite. But the hand-writing was very individual, and very tiny, and it did occur to us that it could be the manuscript of a Brontë novel. Perhaps an early version of one of the known ones, or else an unpublished one.'

'Is that really possible?'

'I don't know. We've been looking into it. There does seem to be a chance — a long shot. Look, what is all this?'

'You see, Superintendent, you've got a reputation of being — well, a bit more at home with these things than the rest of us. I tell you frankly, I'm all at sea. And the fact is, we're very short-staffed at the moment. The PM is visiting areas of high unemployment, and we're drafting in reinforcements everywhere she goes, as you've probably seen —'

'Yes, yes,' I said, 'but what has happened?'

'Miss Wing was attacked, I'm afraid, two nights ago, in her cottage. So far as we can see she must have surprised an intruder. It was a pretty savage attack about the head. Up to now she hasn't regained consciousness. The doctors aren't saying much, but there's a question of brain damage, even if she does come round.'

'Poor old thing. And the manuscript?'

'There's any amount of papers. Letters. Documents. But nothing that looks anything like a novel. Nothing I remember in little tiny handwriting either.'

'I see.'

'You obviously know so much more about it than anyone here. That's why we'd like you to come up.'

'You'd have to talk to the Yard about that.'

'In point of fact, I have done, Mr Trethowan. And the Assistant Commissioner was perfectly willing to second you up here, fairly unofficially, for a week or two, to head the investigation. We'd do all the basic stuff, of course — most of it's done already, in fact. What we need is someone with a good idea of what he might be looking for, and who might be interested in it. You've seen it.

You're up on the background. The question is, are you agreeable?'

Was I agreeable!

'Yes,' I said. 'Yes. Yes.'

CHAPTER 3

PASTORAL VISIT

Jan, it need hardly be said, was desperate to accompany me. It's funny: she has no desire to be at my right hand in cases of insurance frauds, or bankruptcy proceedings, or driving offences. Nor has she shown any desire to be in on shoot-outs with bank raiders, or on the long siege I once had round a block of flats where the IRA were holding hostages. But let there be a bit of glamour, or spice, or merely something different about a case, and she gets her bags packed at once. Luckily, as she very well knew, regulations are quite, nay crystal, clear on this point, and I could, without acrimony, knock the idea bang on the head, once and for all.

'I'll keep in touch by phone,' I said generously.

'I think,' Jan said, stretching meditatively, 'that the time has come to pay another visit to Aunt Sybilla and Aunt Kate.'

'Don't be barmy, woman. We've only been back home a week.'

'Aunt Kate said, as we were leaving, that we could never come too often for her.'

'I remember,' I said. 'Because I repressed with difficulty the impulse to say that we could never come too seldom for me.'

'You are a swine, Perry. If Daniel and I go up there it will be an immense saving in phone bills for you. And you could drop by at the weekend. Spend the odd night.'

I raised my eyebrows and said no more, trusting that Jan would not have the gall to ring Harpenden and suggest it. I just threw a few basic clothes into a travelling bag, and took a taxi to King's Cross to wait for the next train to Milltown. It was a pleasant trip up, marred only by the dreadful meal in the restaurant car (three items on the menu, two of them off — I really don't know how they have the hide . . .). I was met at the station and driven to police headquarters, where I was filled in by Detective-Inspector Capper, the gentle, rather harassed chap to whom I had talked on the phone.

'This is the picture, as far as we have it,' he said, his forehead creased, a sigh in his voice that suggested that the visit of the Prime Minister was the final straw that might break the camel's back of his professional equilibrium. 'The cottage was broken into. Set well back from the road, no near neighbours, child's play. All the doors were secure enough, but as usual the windows were easy as winking.'

'Nothing an amateur couldn't manage?'

'Right. Miss Wing had been down to the one pub in the village, where I gather she went three or four nights a week, just for an hour or so. It was not quite dark when she left there. We presume that when she got back to the cottage she surprised the burglar, intruder, whatever he was, and he hit out — but *very* savagely.'

'Poor old thing,' I said. 'She seemed capable, but not the sort who'd hurt a fly. Anything interesting in her background?'

'Not really. For the last thirty years she had been a mistress at Broadlands — private girls' school near Harrogate. Bit snobby, but a thoroughly good school, sensible people in charge.'

'Clean slate there, naturally?'

'Oh, of course. She'd have been out on her little pink

ear if not. They're very concerned and shocked, naturally. According to them Miss Wing was totally upright, responsible, common-sensical. Probably was. We've no reason to think otherwise.'

'That was certainly the impression she made on my wife and me,' I said.

'Good. Well, she inherited a lot of stuff from a friend and distant relation, who died in January.'

'Rose Something-or-other.'

'Rose Carbury. Books, records, personal mementoes— and apparently this mass of papers. I presume she told you something about that, did she? Did she say that this manuscript, if it existed, was part of this inheritance?'

'Yes, she did. And certainly one page of it existed, because she showed it to us. It looked perfectly authentic—I couldn't go further than that.'

'Good. It's not very likely she'd take up forging in her twilight years, is it? But it's obviously something we have to keep in mind. Now, the fact is that we know that after she had talked to you, she dropped hints to other people. Nothing much, but she certainly did talk about the thing—in the pub, and so on. Silly woman.'

'As it turned out,' I conceded. 'And I certainly warned her about keeping something potentially valuable in her cottage. But she could hardly have been expecting something like this to happen—nobody would. And she wouldn't, I suspect, have realized its value herself. When she gave these hints, did she say what she thought it might be?'

'She may have. So far all I've heard is that she said she "had reason to think she might have inherited a *quite* valuable manuscript" with her friend's things.'

'Hmmm. Quite vague. On that basis they'd hardly know what to look for. Do you know if she got around to consulting an expert?'

'We haven't got as far as that. That'll be for you. The

cottage is all yours. The boys have been over it, of course. You can see their report as soon as you like, but there's precious little in it. The only fingerprints are Miss Wing's own, apart from some old ones on the inherited stuff that are pretty clearly the dead relative's. The window, as I said, was such a piece of cake that there's little to suggest whether it was an amateur or a professional job: kids learn that sort of thing in school these days.'

'And was the manuscript the only thing taken?'

'With Miss Wing in a coma it's difficult to say. We've had a friend in to look round, and as far as she can see nothing has been touched in the rest of the house. But of course she has no idea of what exactly there was in the stuff Miss Wing inherited. The room with those papers in wasn't ransacked, as you will see, but since it was there that she was found, naturally it was there that we concentrated our attention.'

So that was that. I was given a car for the duration, and drove out to Hutton-le-Dales. I found the cottage without any difficulty, because there was a police car outside it. It was, as Miss Wing had said, down a lane from the little main street. I put the car into reverse and drove along to the Dalesman. Bill Martin's wife was fully recovered, and I managed to get a room for the next few days. Then I walked back to the cottage in the early evening sunlight. I introduced myself to the constable on duty—a heavy chap of forty or so, pleasant enough, but not giving the impression he was ever going to make the big time in the Police. I told him I could take over at the cottage for the next day or two, and sent him back to his job of protecting the Prime Minister from hordes of stone-throwing unemployed youth—a job which must involve a delicate balance of lack of sympathy. Then the cottage was mine.

It was really two cottages put together: two two-up-two-downers, in fact. Together they made a nice-sized dwelling for a single person, set well back from the main road, and with a garden which must recently have been a wilderness, but which showed signs of determined effort to bring it round. I suspected Miss Wing had originally acquired the left-side cottage, and only more recently the right-side one. The left one had been decorated, by an enthusiastic but amateur hand, in a conventional, pleasant way. The living-room was comfortable, with old, sat-in furniture. There was a black and white television, and an elderly gramophone with a surprisingly large collection of records: no doubt partly inherited from Rose Carbury. The bookshelves were at the far end of the room, and I went over to inspect them.

The books seemed to be divided into two lots — Miss Wing's own, and those she had inherited. The cousin's were a fairly conventional collection of classics, ancient and modern, in undistinguished editions. Hardly interesting — the sign of a well-read woman, but not one of any individual taste. Miss Wing herself had a lot of books of travel, some school text-books, many volumes on cookery and embroidery. There was only one book of poetry — not Emily Brontë, but Emily Dickinson — another young lady one would not take along to the Annual Police Ball. No sign, then, that Miss Wing had had any previous interest in the Brontë family. There were a few favourite novels, all modern: *South Riding*, *Mrs Palfrey at the Claremont*, Olivia Manning. Later I was to find the cousin's copy of *Wuthering Heights* by Miss Wing's bed upstairs.

There had been a connecting door let into the wall of the living-room, which led through into the little hallway of the right-hand cottage, and thence through to the other living-room. That room was very different. The wall-paper was musty, and of a hideous cheap design. Quite a bit of furniture seemed to have been dumped here, pending redecoration. But that was not what one noticed. The room had been taken over by a large trunk and several cardboard boxes, the containers of the family papers that Miss Wing had inherited. The Yorkshire police had been very careful in their investigations, and it was possible to see that Edith Wing had gone systematically about her work on the papers, as one would have expected. Gradually the papers had come to take over the room.

The cardboard boxes, for example, had been nearly emptied, and the various items stacked in piles around the room, on the furniture or the floor. Some were neatly tied up with string or ribbon. There was a series of letters written in the eighteen-nineties from 'Your loving sister Amy' to her 'Dearest Louise'. There were documents relating to the sale of a manor house in the East Riding, in the early years of the century. There were photograph albums, birth and marriage certificates, three sad War Office telegrams from the First World War. There was material here for a detailed family history (of which Emily Brontë, who was fascinated by family, would surely have approved). But it was all much too late in date to be of much interest to me. I turned my attention to the centrepiece of the room, the trunk.

Here we were much further back. The little piles around the trunk related to the eighteen-fifties and -sixties. There were letters from Mrs Robinson, now Lady Scott, to her daughters. These made my heart thump: here one was in direct contact with one of the players in the Brontë saga — the destroyer of Branwell (or the innocent victim of his unlawful advances, depending on whom you wanted to believe). I could not forbear untying the packet and glancing at their contents. From the earlier letters I had a feeling of coldness — of egotism masking itself in conventional expressions of love, concern, motherly admonition. The later letters had a hint of querulousness, a genteel whine: they seemed to ask, between the lines, why the girls weren't better daughters, and seemed unaware of the obvious answer.

There was another interesting pile of letters from Lady Scott's solicitor, concerning her threat of libel action against Mrs Gaskell and George Smith, her publisher. Mrs Gaskell had been foolish enough, in her biography of Charlotte, to print the account of Branwell's dismissal from his post at the Robinsons' exactly as she had heard it from Charlotte, which meant the account of the affair that Branwell put out for family consumption. Mrs Gaskell added a fine paragraph or two of moral outrage at the conduct of the 'wretched woman' who now 'goes flaunting about to this day in respectable society; a showy woman for her age; kept afloat by her reputed wealth.' Very understandable, even admirable, but not something one could get away with even today, unless one is the fiercely moralistic editor of *Private Eye*. In Victorian days, it was legal suicide. Lady Scott had all the cards in her hand, and would not be content with anything less than a grovel. Mrs Gaskell grovelled.

But the neat piles around the trunk were not all. In the bottom of it was a disorder of papers not yet sorted. I knelt down by it and scuffled around. Odd pages which had fallen out of lengthy documents, various keepsakes such as childish drawings and dried flowers falling to pieces, even a fob watch. I was just giving up when my tumbling about in the debris of past loves and losses turned up riches. My eye caught the signature at once, and I drew it carefully forth. It was the second page of a letter, and it had obviously fallen apart from the other section of the folded sheet. But it provided, even in its fragmentary state, the first direct link with one of the Brontës:

care of it for me. I trust in God, and hope for a few
more years of life yet, not only that I may accomplish

the many schemes I have in my mind, to do good while I may, but also for Charlotte's sake. However, if this be not His will, I bow to it.

Please accept, dear Mary, my assurance of the great happiness it gave me to see you again, and believe that you have the warmest good wishes of your friend and governess

Anne Brontë

I wanted to jump up and shout a *Eureka* that would be heard all the way to Milltown. All right—this was not evidence. Certainly not the police court evidence I was talking about earlier. There was nothing to indicate what the Robinson girl or girls were to take 'care of' for Anne. But it was one piece of beautiful significance in the whole jigsaw puzzle. It showed that Anne, in her last illness (it could surely not have been earlier, because of the reference to Charlotte, without mention of Emily), had in fact entrusted something to her former pupil. If it was in fact the manuscript, it could hardly have been one of her own: she would not have had time to finish anything after writing *The Tenant of Wildfell Hall*. Why should it not be the manuscript of Emily's second novel? She knew that Charlotte deeply disapproved of *Wuthering Heights*. She knew she was also fantastically protective about Emily's reputation. What she could not know, but what perhaps she would not have been surprised at, was that Charlotte would try to suppress one of her own novels, *The Tenant*, after her death. Might she not, fearing that she was about to die, have preferred to trust her sister's manuscript to one of the few people outside the family she had been close to?

I had a strong desire to get on the phone to Jan, and get her to check carefully the events of Anne Brontë's last few months of life. As luck would have it, I sat there on Miss Wing's floor in the gathering twilight, dithering whether to ring from the cottage or go back to the Dalesman and do it. And it was while I was dithering there in the gloom that I heard a scuffle of leaves from outside in the garden.

Quick as a flash I crawled from the musty old living-room into the dark sanctuary of the hallway. There was no glass in the front door of the right-hand cottage, and I stood by the opening between the hall and the left-hand cottage. Somebody was there, all right. I heard careful footsteps. They did not try the doors, no doubt realizing that the police would certainly not leave them unlocked. But I heard faint sounds of the windows being tried, the front windows first of the right-, then of the left-hand cottages.

Then I remembered. When I had first come in, while I was inspecting the bookcases in the main living-room, I had opened a window to let in some air. The main living-room, Miss Wing's main living area, extended the width of the cottage. It had been the back window I had opened. I thought I had closed it again, but certainly not latched it. I waited. The back windows were tried on the right side, without luck. There was a long pause. I imagined him looking in, trying to catch sight of the trunk and documents. Then he struck it rich. I heard the bottom window in the room next to me being cautiously opened. I waited a few seconds, then crept noiselessly forward to the doorway of the living-room.

Inserting itself through the space of the lower window was a large bottom, clad in cheap suiting shiny from use. It came slowly, as if half expecting to be branded. I paused. Then first a left leg, then a right one was swivelled into the room, hands gripped the windowsill, and the top end of the figure began to ease itself through. I could still not see the face, but as it cautiously straightened I observed to my surprise that around its neck it wore a clerical collar.

'Is this just a formal call, or shall I put on the kettle for a cup of tea?' I said.

The head jerked upwards and hit itself on the raised window. The voice, when it spoke, was high and quavery with shock.

'The blessings of the Lord and his prophet Moses be upon you, brother!' it said.

CHAPTER 4

MAN OF GOD

There is this to be said for conventional modes of introduction: you know where you are with them. You stiffen, pull out your mouth to the length that pleasure or anticipation seem to require, hold out a paw and judge the pressure to be applied. The encounter between myself and the reverend, or at any rate clerical, or at any rate dog-collared gentleman, had no such preliminaries. We just stood there, looking at each other. Neither of us, I imagine, liked what he saw. He, though, was obliged to put up a better pretence. He made a valiant attempt to normalize the situation by delving into the inside pocket of his shiny suit, drawing out his wallet, and producing a card.

'Perhaps you'll allow me to introduce myself,' he said, in a quavery voice that was striving to regain normality and clerical fruitiness. I allowed him. The card that I took was dog-eared, almost grimy.

> Revd Amos Macklehose,
> Tabernacle of the Risen Moses,
> Leeds.

'My friends call me Andy,' continued the bulky

figure ingratiatingly.

'Really, Mr Macklehose?' I said, anxious to be on the right footing from the start. I considered the card. It impressed me disagreeably. Totally meaningless, but designed to impress the ignorant. I am not religious, but I do like my religion, or rather other people's religion, to have some respectable theological content. It was clear that Mr Macklehose's was all wind, or all fraud. I looked at Mr Macklehose. He impressed me disagreeably too — very disagreeably. He was overweight, in his late forties, with full lips, cunning eyes and greasy hair, thinning, but smarmed across his pate. He smiled appeasingly at me, and rubbed his hands with that false good-fellowship that is worse than enmity.

'Well now,' I said, after regarding him in silence for long enough to augment his nervousness considerably, 'perhaps you'd like to explain how you come to be here. In this manner.'

'Ah yes,' said Amos Macklehose, as if there was nothing he'd like better, 'naturally you'd want to know.'

He took back his card to gain time, and seemed to be working up an air of breeziness. His voice was odd: the basis was middle-class Yorkshire, but there was something else there too that I could not identify. Could it be American? In spite of the breezy bluff, he was sweating as he meditated his explanation. Licking his tongue furtively around his lips, and sweating. All in all, he was as unattractive a specimen of clerical gentleman as you'd be likely to meet!

'Well?' I said.

'Yes. Well, I suppose it must have looked a bit odd,' he said, with an attempt at urbanity. I nodded, and said nothing. The Br'er Possum ploy. It made him still more uneasy and sweaty. But he tried, I'll say that for him.

'Well now, Sergeant — it is Sergeant? — er — well — it's

like this. When I read in the papers about Cousin Edith's terrible accident—'

'Ah—Cousin Edith.'

'That's right. Though quite distant. Not close kin. When I heard about her terrible—well, attack, I suppose I should call it—*dreadful*, the violence in our streets these days, as I'm sure you have cause to know, Inspector . . . Well, when I heard that Cousin Edith had been Set Upon by Thugs, I said to Mother—that's my wife I designate by that name—I said, Judith, I said, we should go and see Cousin Edith when she comes round. It's only natural she'll want to see her own Kin. And we talked it over a little, and sought Divine Guidance together in the usual manner, and then it came to me: there must surely be some little thing of hers from home that Cousin Edith would like to have round her when she Comes To.'

'Are you sure it wasn't some little thing of hers that Cousin Edith was unlikely to find round her when she gets home that interested you?' I asked.

He drew himself up, and aimed at me a magisterial rebuke.

'Are you implying what I think you are implying, Constable? You seem to forget that you are addressing a Man of God.'

'I'm afraid I'm mainly concerned with upholding the law of man,' I said. 'I don't know if there is any biblical warrant for the crime of breaking and entering, but whether or not, that is what I'm thinking of charging you with.'

'You seem to forget, Officer,' he said, rubbing his hands as if kneading very sticky dough, 'that I am Kin to the good lady who owns this property.'

'True,' I said. 'But not close kin, I believe you said. The lady is unfortunately not in a condition to tell us just how close kin she actually considers you.'

'Ah yes, well, technically, as I admitted, we are quite

distant. But we met—the poor lady, and my wife and I—in connection with the Tragic Last Illness of a close cousin of mine, a Miss Rose Carbury. Also a cousin of Miss Wing. We rediscovered the connection then, so to speak. Miss Wing was with her a good deal, nursing her, towards the End. And naturally we were round her a great deal at that time as well.'

'Naturally,' I said. He was impervious to irony, and seemed to get the idea that I might be coming round to his side. Actually his habit of rubbing his hands as if he were wiping grease off them, and of speaking certain words with clerical emphasis, as if they were Holy Writ, was really giving me the gripes.

'Well, now, when Miss Carbury died, in the fullness of time, she left us a great many family things. Heirlooms, I think we might call them. Because we have been in the past a Prominent Yorkshire Family, Inspector. Looked Up To. Actually, these heirlooms should have been ours many years ago, we being the Senior Branch. Unfortunately, the Dad having gone to America when I was hardly more than a boy, we had dropped out of sight, not to mention the Dad having been less close to Cousin Rose than I would have liked. Kith is kith, I always say. So it was only when Mother and I came back to Yorkshire that we became in any way intimately associated.'

'Oh? And when was that?'

'Nine years ago, come August. I was Planting the Seed in Winnipeg when the Lord called me to Leeds.'

'The Lord seems to call you to some rotten places. Have you been a clergyman all your adult life?'

'Pretty much. Pretty much. The Dad received the Call in California, back in 1951. I was fortunate enough to be similarly Called in 1960. The Dad was most affected. He's still alive, you know, still Shepherding the Faithful in Los Angeles and Santa Barbara. And I'm pleased to say we have found fertile soil here in Yorkshire. Yes, indeed.

Oh, dear, yes.'

'And have you remained close to Miss Wing since Rose Carbury's death?'

'Ah well, yes—and no. In *spirit*, certainly. Affliction brings people together in spirit, as I'm sure you know, Officer. But seeing as how she is distantly Kin, it seems a pity we have not seen more of each other. Consolidated our closeness, as you might say. I said as much to Mother, when I read of the attack. Mother, I said, we must see what we can do for poor Miss Wing. This is just the sort of Sad Eventuation that the Lord sends in order to bring people closer together.'

I have known people who disliked clergymen as a race because they saw them as preying on people in times of distress and bereavement. It certainly did seem to be going it a bit to believe that the Lord had had Edith Wing bashed on the head in order to bring her closer to Amos Macklehose.

'Well, Mr Macklehose,' I said, 'I can doubtless find you any time I want to, and I shall certainly want to. For the moment the best thing is probably to send you on your way. I need hardly say there is no question of anything being removed from this house—beyond what has already been removed. I suppose you would have no notion of what that might be?'

'None in the world, Inspector.'

'Or of anyone who might have had any special motive for doing Miss Wing harm?'

'No, indeed. Indeed, *no*. A harmless spinster lady, and a true friend and kind nurse in times of distress. Who could find a motive for violence in the blameless life of such a one? You must look to the violence of the age, Superintendent. The inborn seed of wrath. Only last night on the television—our Tabernacle congregation has after much heart-searching and prayer come to the conclusion that there is no intrinsic reason why television should not be regarded as one of the Gifts of God—'

'Really? I can think of any number.'

'—last night on television we saw gangs of Youth, Charioteers of Beelzebub, pelting the Prime Minister, one of the Frailer Vessels, with stones, and with eggs, nay even tomatoes. An ugly sight, Inspector. As I said to Mother at the time, I am far from unsure that we are not entering the Sixth Night foreseen in the *Revelation of St John*.'

'Well, Mr Macklehose,' I sighed, repressing the desire to ask for a precise citation of the relevant passage in *Revelation*, 'if you will just take yourself off—'

'You must,' Amos Macklehose pronounced, as if he were awarding the star prize at Bingo, 'you must come and meet Mother. Mother is waiting in the car like the patient Griselda (*Second Book of Kings*). I insist you meet her, Superintendent. You are a man to appreciate her Quality.'

Unwilling to let this chance go by, I allowed him to hurry me out of the cottage. Not so fast, though, that I didn't lock both the window and the doors behind me. One never knew what other Mackleheses might be lurking around in the undergrowth.

Amos of that ilk enthused about his topic all the way down to the gate.

'My Judith, Superintendent, is a woman in a thousand. A jewel beyond price, a pearl in a sow's ear. She is, I can tell you. I don't know what I would have done without her!'

I was a bit uncertain as to what he had done *with* her. I could well imagine that the Reverend Macklehose was on to any number of unsavoury lurks, but if so the resulting income was not lavished on his person: the frayed cuffs of his suit, no less than its shiny seat, did not bespeak prosperity. We went through the gate, and he pointed to the car, fifty yards down the lane.

'Have trouble finding a parking place?' I asked nastily.

He began kneading bread again, frenetically.

'Ah, Mother,' said Amos Macklehose, as we finally drew up beside the car. 'I've got a treat for you. I want you to meet Inspector—'

'I said you didn't ought to have,' said a sepulchral voice. 'I said you didn't ought to have, and I was right.'

The Reverend Macklehose's jewel beyond price was a hard-featured, doom-ridden sort of woman, predestination breathing from her nostrils. She barely acknowledged my presence, but remained staring ahead at the landscape through the car windscreen. She had a thin line of lip, set permanently to disapproval, and a marvellous brown felt hat of the sort everybody's North Country auntie wore thirty years ago. I thought they made a lovely couple.

'You're quite right, Mrs Macklehose, that your husband didn't ough—that he shouldn't have broken into Miss Wing's cottage,' I said. 'You're obviously a woman of principle.'

'I know what's Right,' she said. 'I know what's Right and I say so.' She sniffed and kept looking ahead, but I thought she was thawing towards me a bit.

'Mother saw a good deal of Cousin Edith,' said Amos Macklehose, still uneasy with the conversation and rubbing his hands as if he were a garage mechanic. He looked at me ingratiatingly the while, his head cocked like one of our less appealing feathered friends. 'Saw her most days in dear Cousin Rose's last illness. United they tended her, you might say.'

'She did her duty, I'll say that for her,' pronounced Judith Macklehose. She added, as if as an afterthought, though it was not that: 'Though I've no doubt she had her reasons.'

'Mother!' said Amos Macklehose.

'Really?' I probed. 'You thought she had her reasons?'

'I'm not saying there was anything Wrong, mind you,'

said the charming Judith. 'But Cousin Rose leaving all her personal things away from her nearest Kin is something I'll never understand. I just think it was Funny.'

Judith Macklehose was clearly one of those people for whom funny is never funny-peculiar, let alone funny ha-ha, but always funny-suspicious.

'I'd gathered they were very old friends,' I ventured.

'Oh, *friends*,' said Judith Macklehose, disposing of friendship with a mighty sniff. 'Still, if Edith Wing collected her pile, she worked for it, I'll say that. I'd be the last to begrudge it to her. *Particularly*,' she intoned, with great emphasis, 'particularly in view of what has befallen her.'

She didn't actually use the word retribution, but the word was definitely hanging in the air.

'You've no idea who might have done such a thing—attacked her in this brutal way?'

'Oh no. We'd had no contact with her, not since the funeral, had we, Amos? We weren't privy to her private life, dear me no. Mind you—we did hear . . .'

'Yes?'

'Well, one of our New Israelites—a member of our Tabernacle—comes from here, from Hutton. Three buses there, three buses back, every Sunday without fail. You won't find *that* sort of faith in the Anglicans! Anyway, Fred Hebblethwaite, he told us that since she'd come here, she'd got very fond of a boy—'

'Black!' intoned Amos Macklehose.

'A black boy,' agreed Judith Macklehose, her eyes clearly seeing the brand of Cain. 'He comes to do the garden for her, so they say. Fourteen! Not, of course, that there's anything *in* it. But I do say it's funny . . .'

'We know about blacks, from Los Angeles,' Mr Macklehose assured me, rubbing his greasy hands in an agony of sincerity and insultingly including me in on his remarks with an implicit assumption that as a policeman I would agree. 'Can't walk the streets these days without getting attacked. Brutal thugs. We've had to be strict in our Tabernacle. Not admitted. Of course they'll go to anything with a bit of Enthusiasm.'

'So if you're looking for a likely suspect,' his lovely wife assured me, 'it's my belief you need look no further. Making no judgments, of course.'

'Of course,' I said. 'Naturally not. So you both have lived in Los Angeles, have you?'

'Yes. Yes indeed!' enthused Amos. 'Met there, did we not, Judith? So in spite of the Sin and the Shame — and there *is* Sin, there *is* Shame — Los Angeles will always be a very special place for us. As you might say, The Promised Land. And the Dad did very nicely there too!'

'I don't detect any American in your accent,' I said to Judith.

'I went,' she intoned, 'on an Exchange Visit.'

'That's it!' enthused Amos, as if she had just produced a spiritual revelation. 'Mother was a British Israelite then, weren't you, Mother? And you exchanged with a family of British Israelites in California. Nineteen fifty-five it was. After we met you switched — or rather your earlier Call became subsumed as you might say in your new Call. Since then we've never looked back. Twelve years serving the Lord and his prophet Moses in Winnipeg, and now nine years in similar joyful service in Leeds. It makes you humble, indeed it does. A high calling, Officer, a joyful burden. Once the Word is known, it spreads like wildfire. You should come to one of our meetings, you know. Your life could be Transformed.'

'I'm afraid I have no time to be Transformed in the immediate future,' I said. 'Though I certainly might be paying you a visit. For the moment I've got a job of work to do. I'll say good-night to both of you.'

'The peace of the Lord God and the benediction of the

Prophet Moses be upon you, Constable,' chirped out Amos Macklehose blithely. He jumped into the driving seat, slammed her into reverse, and drove erratically backwards towards the main street of Hutton-le-Dales. As he did so, he came within an ace of running over my toe, I swear deliberately. There was a manic smile on his face as he receded into the distance.

I stood there watching as the car jerkily made it to the main road, and drove off in the direction of Leeds. I swore as I stood there to have the Reverend Amos Macklehose, preferably with his Pearl of Great Price beside him, up in the dock on some charge before this case was over. Already I could probably have him under the Race Relations Act, but that was much too namby-pamby in its penalties for my purposes. I wanted Amos to fry.

Pending which culinary treat, I fetched my bag from the Dalesman and spent the night in Edith Wing's cottage. I didn't want evidence destroyed or valuables stolen by any other marauding clergymen that night.

CHAPTER 5

MATTERS ACADEMICAL

The next morning first thing, after a rather uneasy night spent in Miss Wing's spare bedroom, I rang to the Milltown police and arranged for a police guard to be resumed on the cottage. The Prime Minister was about to depart, to spread economic theory o'er the unemployed of Liverpool, so things in the area were returning more to normal. I also suggested that they do something to strengthen the locks on the cottage windows.

Me, my next stop was Milltown, but before I went I got

on the telephone to the secretary of the English Department at the University there.

'I wonder if you could help me?' I said, not identifying myself as police. 'Could you tell me who it would be best to see in the Department with a question about the Victorian novel?'

'Oh, you're the second this week to ask that,' she replied.

'Really? Who was the other?'

'I don't remember the name. A lady, it was. Anyway, it's a rather difficult question.'

'Oh?'

'Well, by rights, by etiquette if you like, I ought to say Professor Gumbold. He is the senior man, and head of department, in name anyway . . .'

'Yes?'

'The trouble is, he's—' she lowered her voice—'quite gaga. I mean, absolutely. There's some here who seem gaga but aren't, there's some who don't seem gaga but are. He's gaga and it shows. Even the students have noticed. So there's really no point in sending you along to him with a question. You'll get a lecture on Carlyle's ethical philosophy. It was writing a book on Carlyle sent him round the twist. I can only suggest to you what I suggested to the other lady—that you go along to Timothy Scott-Windlesham.'

'He's not gaga?'

'No-o,' she said. 'He's not *gaga* . . .'

The tone of her voice was not calculated to make the salivary glands run in anticipation. I could see I was in for a difficult morning. But then, I hadn't been looking forward to it anyway. I must go a bit carefully here. There's nothing irritates me more than people who condemn whole professions: the police are pigs, all soldiers are fascists—that kind of thing. I call it jobism, and it's quite as bad as racism. Still, I have to say that I have not greatly liked the academics I have come in contact with in the course of my life. Of course, you could say I don't as a rule see them at their best: mostly when I've met them it has been in connection with some kind of offence or other—thieving from bookshops, mostly, or sexual offences of a slightly ludicrous nature. But I have to admit that they have seemed the most snivelling, self-important scraps of humanity you can imagine, and as windy and whiney a bunch as ever demanded special privileges without doing anything to deserve them. Of course they might be quite charming in their natural environment. Anyway, it was with this sort of foreboding that I set off for Milltown.

The University of Milltown, it is said and widely believed, came into being as a result of a hold-up on British Rail. One day back in the 'sixties or early 'seventies the train containing the then Prime Minister, Mr Wilson or Mr Heath (folk memory is uncertain which, and in retrospect they do seem increasingly indistinguishable), came to a full stop just outside Milltown, and the Great Man—whichever—on the way from a party conference here to a bye-election rally there sat for twenty minutes looking out at the long rows of grime-encrusted houses, built in long monotonous terraces, and at the gimcrack office blocks and the tightly-packed skyscrapers containing council flats (built, we now learn, due to some failure of socio-architectural theory). And the Great Man, forcibly becalmed into contemplation, turned to his wife, or the underling who was with him, and he said: 'This is a town with absolutely nothing.' And after another ten minutes of hold-up and painfully enforced thought the Great Man had pronounced: 'What it needs is a university.' And so that is what it got.

Like so many ideas of our modern Great Men, this one could have done with a bit of thinking through. For the

University of Milltown had not exactly prospered.
Student enrolment was precarious. Even as a staging-post
on the road from school to unemployment it was not
popular. Why, after all, fritter away three years in such
an environment as Milltown when gayer, livelier, more
beautiful surroundings are equally available to you for
frittering in? The North Country young called it the
University of Last Resort. Other new universities had
made their mark: you went to one because you were
bright, to another because you were revolutionary, to a
third because you were over-sexed. You went to Milltown
because it was there. There were whispers of closure, but
the fact is that it's confoundedly difficult to make
academics unemployed. Even the architects had shown
signs of faint-heart and lack of conviction. At least the
other new universities have a certain bold awfulness — a
brave Scandinavian fist thrust in the face of comfort,
convenience and pleasurable living. The University of
Milltown looked like the rest of Milltown. Two or three
blocks that could be council offices, or the business
premises of some shaky concern or other; several large
hangar-like constructions that could be chain-store cash-
and-carry warehouses; some builder's sheds that no one
had bothered to demolish. It hadn't led to a lively
environment. Even in the early 'seventies the students
hadn't been militant. They explained at NUS conferences
that they were too depressed. Everybody understood.

I had been enjoying the drive up to then, through
marvellous countryside, and I'd been singing bits of
Verdi. I stopped when I got to the campus.

At any rate you could say it was well signposted.
Fingerposts everywhere telling me where to go, as if it
were some much-visited stately home. I left my car in the
car park, which was miles from anywhere, and I walked
past rugby fields, football pitches and finally tennis
courts. A couple of chaps were hitting a ball around

dispiritedly. A placard on the gate announced 'North of England Championships, Leeds, June 15th-20th.' It didn't look as if they'd make the grade. I finally found 'English Department' on one of those signposts (like those on the South Bank in London) that tell you where absolutely everything is, but somehow leave you more confused than ever about how to get there. I went wrong twice, but finally located the English Department on the third and fourth floors of one of the blocks that looked like local council offices. There was no lift, and as I started up the stairs I was nearly crushed into the ground by a sudden rush of students from a lecture-room, all of them apparently desperate for air. I tell you, I didn't like this place long before I got to the English Department.

Which, when I did get there, proved to be a large central square, windowless, lit with neon tubes one of which was flickering aggravatingly. Off it were corridors leading to offices. There was one notice-board for official notices, another for student activities. There were no student activities. The official one had a list of names and rooms of staff members, little bits of paper advertising cancelled lectures, and various broadsheets suggesting to students a variety of activities and attractions. Some of them were relevant to their studies: contemporary literature courses here, there and everywhere, all of them addressed by Malcolm Bradbury and Ian McEwan. Some of them were rather odd, such as another advertisement for the tennis championships, and another suggesting an overland safari to Australia as a suitable way of spending the summer vacation. Could the staff be wanting to get rid of them?

By the notice board was an office, and as I stood reading I heard a high voice shrieking: 'I am Professor of English and head of this department, and I insist . . .' I looked at the name on the door. It was Gumbold. I was grateful to the secretary for warning me off. I strayed down the corridor in search of Timothy Scott-Windlesham. The notice-board had said he was in Room 423, but the numbering system, nominally consecutive, seemed to have been applied on a plan that could only have been the work of a lunatic or a mathematician. There was hardly a soul about. When finally I found Room 423 there was talk going on inside. I knocked tentatively. There was sudden silence, and then the door opened a fraction and a pale face peered out. It said in a high voice: 'Ten minutes. I'm busy. No, twenty.' Then it popped in again.

I walked away. I wondered how one filled in twenty minutes in an English Department. At the end of the corridor the architect, in a burst of generosity, had allowed a window. By it was an open door, with voices coming through. The label on the door said, in small letters, 'staff room'. The staff of the English Department, presumably. I went towards it, and poked my head around the door. There were four people in the room, lounging around with cups in their hands. A stocky woman with ugly dark hair and a light moustache glared at me.

'Are you a student?'

'No.'

'Oh—sorry.' She looked genuinely contrite, as if she'd called me a rude name. 'You never know these days. We get a lot of older people under these retraining schemes.'

Now she really had insulted me. 'I am not an older person,' I said. 'As a matter of fact, my wife has just finished her degree at Newcastle.'

'Really?' She looked around at the others. 'I say, do you remember when Newcastle was absolutely the end of the road, academically? Since this place was built it's practically Oxbridge.' She looked back at me. 'Like a cup of coffee?'

'Love one.'

'It's instant,' said a burly, bearded, aggressive type, who seemed to flourish the word like a banner and dare me to say that I only drank percolated.

'That's what I like,' I said. 'Just as I prefer my tea in bags and my orange juice from tins with additives. Do I pass?'

'Oh God, a funny one,' said a languid someone in the corner. 'Thank God you're not a student. The funny ones are the ones I can't stand the most.'

At this point a thin, silent, middle-aged man with a stoop and an unhealthy skin got up and walked out without a word. I looked at him suspiciously, and suddenly realized it was someone I'd arrested long ago in my beat-walking days for exposing himself in the Charing Cross Road.

'What,' asked the young woman with the faint moustache, 'are you actually wanting?'

'What I was actually wanting was a talk with Mr Scott-Windlesham.'

'Lucky old you. Here's your coffee.'

'Thank you. Oh — real milk. A luxury.'

'Oh God,' said Languid. 'An ironist. You'll get on well with Timothy. He's rather fond of the old irony himself.'

'Flat-irony, mostly,' said Moustache. 'Well, your treat is all ahead of you. What can we do for you the while? Recite Shakespeare sonnets?'

'It's actually a question about Victorian literature I'm seeing him about,' I said. 'I spoke to your secretary, and she said Professor Gumbold was . . . that he had . . .'

'Cracked up,' said Beard. 'Fallen over the intellectual precipice.'

'Enrolled as a life student of the Higher Lunacy,' said Languid.

'It's an awful thing,' said Moustache contemplatively, 'when a perfectly average, plodding, third-rate academic goes bang off his head. The collapse of a brilliant mind has something grand, something King Leary about it. The spectacle of Gumbold mad is just dreary and ludicrous.'

'It's we who suffer,' said Languid. 'His lectures used to be competent and dull as ditchwater, and the students didn't listen. Now they're totally gaga and the students don't go. Not a ha'porth of difference for them. But it's we who have to put up with his tantrums and lunacies. And he's still supposed to be in charge of the department.'

'His psychiatrist,' said Beard, 'suggested his mind needed something restful and soothing in the academic line, to calm it down after all that Carlyle. He's always been a hypochondriac, and we suggested a project on asthmatics in literature. It's not working out too well as yet.'

'There are no asthmatics in literature,' said Moustache. 'It's an intrinsically unliterary illness, without the romance of tuberculosis. Well—that's our life's burden. I suppose you were told, *faute de* Gumbold, to go along to Timothy?'

'That's right. Is he your other Victorian man?'

'Person,' said Moustache.

'I *suppose* you could say so,' said Beard grudgingly. 'What do you want to ask him about?'

'The Brontës.'

Moustache hooted with laughter. 'You won't get much change out of Timothy on the Brontës. Timothy is a Meredith man. And why is Timothy a Meredith man?'

'Because,' said Languid, 'if you study a minor aspect of a great writer—say Fielding's plays, or something— there's always the danger someone will read one of them and want to discuss it with you. Whereas Meredith is a respectable name, with acres of novels that nobody has read.'

'And if,' said Moustache, 'by some remote chance

somebody comes along who *has* read *Harry Richmond* or *The Egoist*, you say: "Oh, that's the *popular* Meredith. I can't think I'll be spending too much time on *that*." That's the principle Timothy works on. Because he's a secretive little squirt, and whether he's actually done any work on Meredith or not I don't know, but he certainly has no wish to talk about it with any of us. And he absolutely loathes the Brontës.'

'I don't know,' said Beard. 'I saw him buying a copy of *Wuthering Heights* in the bookshop the other day.'

'What kind of lecturer in Victorian literature is it who doesn't own a copy of *Wuthering Heights*?' demanded Moustache, with a good deal of reason. 'He loathes them. When he took over Gumbold's novel course he struck them right off, first thing he did. They're too popular for our Timmy. And too local. He calls them Yorkshire Home Industries Limited. Our Timothy is a great cosmopolitan. So if you're bringing him a problem on the Brontës, you're barking up the wrong tree.'

'The right metaphor would be leaning on a broken reed,' said Beard, 'Timothy bearing such an uncanny resemblance to a broken reed. You'd do much better to go to someone in Leeds or Sheffield.'

'Tell me,' I said, 'Mr Scott-Windlesham — or is it Doctor — ?'

'Mr,' said Moustache firmly.

'Mr Scott-Windlesham hasn't mentioned, has he, a visit from a lady last week — a lady with a manuscript?'

'No. But then, he probably wouldn't. He fraternizes, but he never confides, our Timmy. What sort of manuscript was it?'

'Well, that I can't say exactly, but it's quite long, and it's in very small handwriting —'

'Ho-ho,' said Beard. 'Now I see where we've been going. Brontë juvenilia, by any chance?'

'Possibly,' I said diplomatically. 'As far as I know,

nobody with any expertise has looked at it.'

'Bound to be a fake,' said Moustache, 'otherwise someone would have been on to it years ago. Even twenty years ago people used to give their right hand for those little books. Today there's just nothing on the market.'

'Bound to be a fake,' agreed Beard. 'Or one of those American collectors would have had it years ago. Or perhaps old Tetterfield in Bradford.'

They all tittered.

'Who's that?' I asked.

'An absolutely manic librarian. Head of the West Riding Regional Library. Has a mania for collecting everything about Yorkshire writers. J.B. Priestley's tobacconist's bills, John Braine's underwear. He's just mad to get together a collection of Brontë stuff of his own, naturally, but he's come on to the market too late, and there's practically nothing around. He's got a bit of a private income to back him up, but it's not big enough to get him any of the really high-price stuff. He's as gaga as old Gumbold, as a matter of fact, but it doesn't notice so much in a librarian.'

'If the lady had come along to you, would you have recommended her to go to him?'

They all sat around the table in thought. Finally it was Moustache who spoke.

'Well, it would have depended what she wanted, wouldn't it? If she wanted to sell—and she'd have to be crazy not to—I'd have said call in the experts, but deposit the thing in your bank while you're waiting, because it will take time.'

'More or less what I said,' I put in.

'On the other hand, if she was the philanthropic type who wanted to make it generally available and so on, then either she should give it to the Brontë Parsonage Museum or to some library. The British Library would be an obvious choice, or maybe the Brotherton in Leeds.'

'I wonder if that's what Mr Scott-Windlesham recommended,' I said.

'Timothy? Timothy's first thought would be: what's in it for me? That you can be quite sure of. I can't quite see what there could be in it for him, though.'

'Unless,' said Beard, 'he did her in, and kept the manuscript for himself. Supposing he had the nerve.'

'Why all the questions, anyway?' asked Languid, languidly.

'I'm Police. The lady was savagely beaten around the head and the manuscript taken. Dear me. Twenty minutes is up. Thanks for the instant. I'd better get along to see Mr Scott-Windlesham.'

CHAPTER 6

EXPERT ADVISER

I trusted my last words had left them goggling in there. Or perhaps Beard had meant the suggestion perfectly seriously anyway. It is not only in academic circles that people will habitually believe the worst of a colleague. Policemen are always being accused of brutality, and I remember only once totally and entirely refusing to entertain an allegation against one of my mates. And he turned out to have beaten a left-wing demonstrator to pulp with a lead-weighted truncheon.

Anyway, I needn't have worried that I had missed my appointment with Timothy Scott-Windlesham. When I came out into the corridor his door was just opening. As I walked towards his office the door was shut firmly again, for the conversation to be concluded. I loitered around, pretending to an inexhaustible interest in the names of the staff-members on the various doors. I had heard of

none of them. Milltown, it seemed, did not produce telly
luminaries, quiz-show panellists, part-time novelists or
Parliamentary candidates. Vegetation was sparse in
Milltown as a whole, but it looked as if that was what was
going on in its English Department.

Eventually the conversation was concluded, and two
large fair men emerged from Scott-Windlesham's office
and, without words of farewell, marched away down the
corridor. Remembering the wounding conjecture of
Moustache, I wondered if they were adult students, the
only breed of student that seemed to flourish in Milltown.
Training themselves for a more cultured form of
unemployment, probably. I let a moment or two elapse,
and then went and knocked on the door.

'Oh — come *in*,' said an irritable thin voice.

Timothy Scott-Windlesham was sitting at his desk, but
he swung his chair round to face the door as I entered,
presumably so as to look like a writer interrupted in mid-
œuvre. He was middling in height, but thin and hollow-
chested. He was pasty in complexion, or at any rate he
was pasty now, as if he had just been sick: the general
effect was of an uncooked dumpling. His hair was long
and straight and lank, and had been finger-combed
across his head, no doubt in a moment of stress. His tie
was askew, his shirt unironed, and he grabbed a packet
from his desk and stuck a filter-tip in his mouth.

'Oh, you. You were here before, weren't you? What is
it?'

Gracious little twit. The idea that manners maketh
man clearly went out of the educational system before he
went into it. I suited my behaviour to his, and took the
one easy chair in his office, without being asked.

'Mr Scott-Windlesham? I'm sorry to trouble you, since
it's clear you're busy. I came because I believe you're an
expert on Victorian literature.'

'Ye-e-es.'

'Isn't Meredith your speciality?'

'Ye-e-e-es' (still more doubtfully).

Experimentally I said: 'I've only read *The Ordeal of Richard Feverel.*'

With push-button precision, Scott-Windlesham replied: 'Oh, that's the *popular* Meredith. I can't say I find that very interesting myself.'

Well, Moustache certainly knew her Timothy Scott-Windlesham. I guessed he was the sort of teacher who is marvellous at communicating his own lack of enthusiasm.

'It wasn't Meredith, actually, I wanted to talk about,' I said. 'Perhaps I'd better introduce myself. I'm a police officer — Superintendent Trethowan.'

Policemen are always imagining that people go white when they introduce themselves. Often they do, but for no reason relevant to the matter in hand. Anyway, I was pretty sure that Scott-Windlesham went a further shade of pastiness at this point. He said nothing, though, and merely goggled at me in an inarticulate and unacademic sort of way. His hands, on the arms of his desk chair, seemed to be almost gripping them. I was forced to go on without any encouragement from him.

'I've come to you because we have a little problem you might be able to help us clear up.' Timothy Scott-Windlesham nodded, looking helpful, and seemed to have managed to swallow his first reactions. 'I believe you had a visit some time last week from a lady with a question about the Brontës.'

Timothy's face fell again, indefinably.

'Ye-e-es.'

'A Miss Edith Wing.'

'Was that the name? It was Marjory — our secretary — who made the appointment. With Professor Gumbold being . . . far from well . . . an awful lot of extra stuff descends on me that ought by rights to be his pigeon. Not that I'm complaining. And of course, though this

Miss Wing wasn't a student, still, I do think one of the things one has to do, perhaps particularly in a place like Milltown, with no old university tradition, is to keep oneself as *open* as possible, to the community at large, I mean, because if we are going to serve any real function *in* the community as a whole — '

He went on in this vein for some time. Perfectly unexceptionable sentiments, but they struck me as blather. We get used to blather, in the police. And I served for a time in the Houses of Parliament. Politicians' blather is to impress, suspects' blather is to gain time. I thought Timothy Scott-Windlesham wanted to gain time. I waited until the flow had dried up.

'And what exactly was it that Miss Wing wanted to see you about?'

'Well, as you said, the Brontës . . .' I sat silent, to force him to go on. I thought it possible he was considering whether to tell an outright lie. If so, he decided against it.'

'She had this little book, you know: tiny pages, minute script, practically unreadable. As far as I remember, she said she'd inherited it. And it was obviously very old — faded, dog-eared, and so on. Though of course that's very easily faked.'

'You thought she might be a forger of some kind?'

Timothy Scott-Windlesham shrugged his hunchy shoulders.

'Just one of the possibilities.'

'And when you had inspected the manuscript, you suggested — ?'

'Well, that it might be — no, wait: I think she brought that up, now I come to think about it. She suggested that it might be a manuscript of one of the Brontës.'

'I see. Did you agree with that?'

'Only in so far as that was certainly one of the possibilities. I wasn't in a position to do any more than that. One would have to be an expert. Of course the Brontës are a fascinating topic, fabulous writers and all that — I meditate a little piece on Emily's French essays in the near future — but I'm not myself a specialist in them. All I could say was that the Brontës were the first names to spring to mind — naturally.'

It would all have been more convincing if I had not just heard his previously expressed opinions on the Brontës. In any case, the cloak of learning seemed to sit uneasily on his meagre frame.

'You don't know of any other writers, then, using that sort of tiny script?'

'No, but as I say, I'm not an expert on holographs, not at all. And of course, there is no guarantee that this was by a *writer*, in the sense you probably intend. Anybody around at that time could have developed a script like that — particularly someone who could not afford to buy a lot of paper.'

Fair point, that. It had occurred to Jan and me too, but I made a mental note not to underestimate Timothy Scott-Windlesham. I entered a caveat, though.

'True enough. But it would be likely to have been a compulsive writer, wouldn't it?'

'Not necessarily. Quite ordinary people, writing letters, wrote two pages on one by writing cross-wise — they turned the paper forty-five degrees and just wrote over what they had just written. Florence Nightingale did, I know.'

'I see. So did you rather pour cold water on the idea?'

'No, no, *no*, Superintendent.' He leaned forward in an agony of goodwill and sincerity. 'Not at all, dear me no. But what I did do was try not to raise false hopes. Surely you can see that that was only kind? Because it would have been an awful let-down if it had turned out to be written by Amelia Smith, a dressmaker's apprentice from Halifax, or something.'

'True. So what did you say?'

'Well, the obvious thing: that what she needed was
an expert, someone with special qualifications in
manuscripts. I thought if I told her to take it to Haworth
that would rather prejudge the affair. So I suggested she
take it along to a librarian, who would know the sort of
person to contact. Then there would be no question of
anyone trying to confirm a preconceived idea.'

'I see. You suggested the university library here?'

'Good God, no. The librarian here's nothing but a sexy
dwarf. He's only interested in grabbing his girls behind
the desk. He wouldn't know a Brontë manuscript from a
ship's log.'

'Where did you recommend she go, then?'

'I don't think I recommended anywhere, but I think I
mentioned Leeds and Halifax. The Brotherton Library at
Leeds is a very respectable collection — oodles of Brontë
stuff, I believe, so they'd certainly be interested.'

'I see. And she accepted this advice?'

Timothy spread out his hands. Women, he seemed to
say. Who can be sure with them? 'So far as I know. She
thanked me, and said it seemed a good idea.'

'And did you talk about this to anyone? Your wife? Any
of your colleagues?'

'I haven't got a wife. We're separated. No, I certainly
didn't mention it to any of my colleagues, as you call
them.'

'Why?'

'For a start, the likelihood was that there was nothing
in it: lost manuscripts don't turn up in trunks every day of
the week, and certainly not Brontë juvenilia. I know
there's mountains of it, but still it did seem more likely
that this was some schoolgirl's gushy attempt at fiction
from back in the nineteenth century somewhere. Then
my dear colleagues would have sniggered like crazy and
put it about that I'd thought a Victorian school-miss's

trash was the work of a Brontë—there's no loyalty here, I'm awfully afraid. So you can be *quite* sure I didn't say a word to any of them.'

'Nor anybody else? You didn't, for example, talk about it over a pint with anyone?'

'You have the oddest idea, Superintendent, of what one talks about over a pint in Milltown.' He smirked. 'It may be all sorts of things, but I assure you it is never literary manuscripts.'

'I take your point. Did Miss Wing say what she would do with the manuscript if it did turn out to be of interest? Sell it? Give it to a library or museum?'

'Really, we had hardly come to that stage—that *would* have been crossing one's bridges. In any case she was consulting me as—God help me—' (here he put on a self-deprecating grin, which twisted his sunken cheeks)—'a literary man, not as a lawyer, or a financial adviser.'

'One last point, and then I'll need to trouble you no longer. Tell me, how much of the manuscript did you get to read?'

'Well, I didn't get to *read* any of it. I mean, it was frightfully difficult to decipher. I just cast my eye over it—you know how it is: I just caught the odd name, because of the capital letters standing out. Mendith Crag, I remember. Ling-something Manor. Somebody called Blackmore, I think. But it was all terribly closely written—the speech not separated off from the rest. It would have taken me *days* to go through the whole thing. I'm a busy man, Superintendent.'

I could take a hint.

'Then I'll take my leave, sir. Thank you very much for all your help.' At the door, I paused. 'You may have been wondering why I've been asking these questions . . .'

Timothy gulped a little.

'Yes. Yes, indeed. I didn't quite like to enquire.'

'Miss Wing was brutally attacked two nights ago.'

'Really? How shocking!'

'And the manuscript was stolen.'

'I see. That explains it. It sounds quite barbaric. Really, one rather hopes it does turn out to be the outpourings of Miss Amelia Smith of Halifax, doesn't one?'

'Not this one, sir. I hope it's a Brontë manuscript. Because I'm going to get it back.'

'Then I wish you good luck. And good morning, Superintendent.'

So that was that. I trudged along the dreary corridors of the English Department. At the big square with the notice-boards, I paused. Professor Gumbold was on the phone again.

'As a member of Faculty and a former Dean, I insist the matter be discussed. My position here is being *undermined* by elements in the Department I can only describe as *seditious*—'

The high-pitched voice went on for some time. A twinge of pity went through me for anyone forced to work under Professor Gumbold. I got myself out of the high-rise block, narrowly escaping once again being trampled underfoot by students escaping from the lecture-room. I trudged over the depressing campus, through the hangars, and the tatty blocks, past the football pitch and the tennis courts, towards my car. It had not been a very revealing interview, but when I set my mind to work, going over it, one or two interesting points emerged.

The first oddity that struck me was that Timothy Scott-Windlesham had not demanded to know why he was being questioned. Anyone would, and an academic, especially, would be likely to stand on his rights. But I had practically had to force the information on to him.

The next thing that struck me was Timothy's mention of juvenilia. This effectively demoted the manuscript to something of secondary interest—a fascinating curiosity,

valuable, but of no great literary worth. Anyone hearing
of an unknown Brontë manuscript would naturally
assume, perhaps, that it was juvenilia. But Timothy
Scott-Windlesham had actually *seen* it, and read bits of
it. The names he remembered — Mendith Crag, Lingdale
Manor, Thomas Blackmore — sounded much more like
the world of the mature Brontë novels than the
overheated worlds of Angria and Gondal they had
invented in childhood, though to be sure Yorkshire did
invade the romantic-improbable nomenclature of those
worlds at times.

And the third thing was the libraries. Leeds and
Halifax no doubt did have excellent libraries. But
Bradford was no further away, and Bradford,
apparently, had a manic collector of Yorkshire literary
manuscripts at its head. What was the name? Tetterfield.
But that library, it seemed, Timothy had not mentioned
at all. Why?

I felt I could easily get interested in Mr Tetterfield.

CHAPTER 7

MAN OF BOOKS

As I drove away from the University of Milltown, without
a regretful backward glance, I felt a prickling in the spine
that meant I had decided I had to see this Tetterfield.
And certainly it could not be said that there were any
other pressing leads that demanded to be followed up,
apart perhaps from the activities, professional and
unprofessional, of the Reverend Amos Macklehose. So I
got out my AA map and discovered that Bradford was
only thirty-five miles or so. Since Hutton-le-Dales could
be taken in with only the smallest of detours, I decided to

drop in there on the way, to see if anything had turned up. It was a gorgeous spring day, and Hutton was looking idyllically peaceful when I drove through it. There was no sign of life at the cottage, but as I opened the gate a figure came round the side of the cottage, wheeling a barrow. It was a boy of thirteen or so, and he grinned cheerily at me as I came into the little garden.

'Hello,' he said. 'I got permission. Are you the one that's investigating the break-in?'

'Yes,' I said. 'And you're the young man who helps in the garden.'

His hair was short and curly, and his skin was just slightly browner than it might be from a fortnight on the Algarve. Even my wife's parents (a charming couple whom you'll meet some time, I expect, though if I were you I wouldn't be in too much of a hurry) would have found it difficult to detect more than the faintest touch of the tarbrush (to use their favourite phrase)—though to do them justice, that touch would be enough: in racial matters they have all the beautiful tolerance of the British urban working-class. No doubt this touch was sufficient too to mark him off in rural Yorkshire—certainly the fact that he was 'coloured' had been carried to the appalling Macklehoses.

'That's me,' said the boy. 'We've got the day off school today, and I thought I'd do a bit for Miss Wing. She'll want it looking all right when she comes out of hospital.' He must have seen a shadow pass over my face, because his forehead crinkled, and he looked up at me. 'She will come out, won't she? She will be all right?'

'We hope so,' I said. 'But she hasn't regained consciousness yet.'

'Oh golly,' he said. 'She mustn't *die*.'

'You get on well with her?'

'Oh yes. She's all *right*. She pays me a bit for the jobs I do in the garden. And she teaches me a bit—about plants and that. She says I've got a gift for natural history. No one else says I've got a gift for anything. She doesn't think the school I go to's any good, doesn't Miss Wing. She says I should be a bo- botanist when I grow up.'

'And will you?'

'Don't know,' he said, grinning. 'It's a while yet, isn't it?'

'Do you know anything about the break-in?' I asked.

'Only what the rest of the village has been saying. Wish I did know something. I'd like to get him. The first I heard about it were next morning — the other kids were talking about it on 't school bus. I got off and walked back, but the place were swarming wi' cops, and Miss Wing were in hospital. I got into hot water over that, at school.'

'What about the day before — or the day before that? Notice anything suspicious in the village?'

'Suspicious? Like what sort of thing?'

'Like strangers, for example.'

'Don't remember,' he said reluctantly, after screwing up his face with effort. 'People drive through here, you know, and sometimes they stop at the pub. I think there may have been some religious people around about then —'

'Religious people?'

'Je-Jehovah's Witnesses, or summat. My Mam shut the door on them. Said we didn't want anything to do wi' that sort o' thing. She said they were foreign.'

So it presumably wasn't Mr Macklehose, or any of his flock. It didn't sound of any significance.

'Well,' I said, 'think about it. And keep your eyes open. Come to me or the constable here if you notice anything at all.'

'Oh, I will,' he said, enthusiastically. 'You've got to get the rotten bastard who did it.'

'I will,' I said. Nothing like confidence for ensuring the

co-operation of the public.

Nothing much was stirring inside the cottage. Through in the kitchen the duty constable, PC Bradley, had seen me talking to the boy and had put on the kettle for a cup of tea.

'Was it all right, letting him do the garden?' he asked, as we sat down at the kitchen table and I pulled out a crumby pork pie I had picked up on the way. 'Our boys went over it very thoroughly after the break-in, and he was keen to get something done.'

'Quite all right. What's his name?'

'Jason Curle,' said Bradley, as if it was the most usual name in the world, which these days I suppose it is. 'The mother's from round here. Picked up that little lot while she was working in Newcastle. Could have had an abortion — should have done, I'd say — but she decided to keep it.'

PC Bradley consigned Jason to oblivion quite unrancorously, but I can't say I shared his confident judgment as to who would have been better not to be born. I didn't pursue the matter.

'Does he have problems here?' I asked. Bradley shrugged.

'Nothing serious, but you know what these small places are like. People talk. Kids'll use anything if they want to be cruel. Miss Wing was very good to him, so they say. By the way, someone who said she was your wife rang.'

'Oh?' I said suspiciously. 'I expect it was my wife, then.'

'Could be. Said would you ring back when you came in. Gave me this number.'

I looked at the slip of paper. It was the number of Harpenden, my family's ancestral pile, now run at a loss by the Northumberland County Council, and visited in droves by people who pretend they want to see the pictures but really want to gape at my appalling family. So Jan had gone 'home', as she had threatened. I got up and went to the phone in a bad temper. She must have been waiting for the call, because she answered at once.

'Hello, Perry. So you see, I did come home.'

'So I gather.'

'Daniel was looking peaky, and I thought he needed a change of air.'

'Daniel was not looking peaky when I left.'

'I fed him Mars bars all the way up. When we got here he was looking like death.'

'You're a monster,' I said cordially. 'An unnatural mother — Clytemnestra, or someone of that sort.'

'He's all right now. Romping around in the gardens with Cristobel and the baby. Well, come on — what has happened? Give me a progress report.'

It was with considerable satisfaction that I balked her.

'I'm back at the cottage having a bite to eat with the duty constable,' I said meaningfully. Jan let out a little groan. She knows the rules. 'Yes, well, you'll have to wait, won't you? But at least you'll be in good company.'

'I had lunch with Aunt Kate,' said Jan.

'Then you're justly punished for your morbid decision.'

'Not at all,' said Jan triumphantly. 'I took along fillet steak. All you need is a modicum of intelligent foresight, you know, Perry.'

I banged down the phone and began collecting some things together.

'Know anything about any door-to-door religious people who were around the village last week?' I asked Bradley.

'Someone did mention them,' he said. 'Witnesses, or Adventists, or one of those loony sects. Foreign they were — Swedes, or Norwegians, or some such. I didn't pay much attention. They're crazy, but they're not dangerous.'

I nodded. 'Know anything about someone called Tetterfield? A head librarian at Bradford.'

'Librarian?' said Bradley, much as one might say Christadelphian, or Flat-Earther. I gave up. Librarians clearly did not enter into either his personal or his professional line of vision. I certainly seemed to be mingling with the non-professional criminal in this case. I left the cottage, waved to young Jason, and took off for Bradford.

Bradford is a mixture of odd nice bits, with odd nasty ones somewhat outnumbering them, and it isn't somewhere you linger, except that it's easy to get lost in a lot of hilly back streets. I expended a lot of time and patience before I located the West Riding Regional Library. It was a research library, designed to serve the whole of West Yorkshire, and it was situated some way away from the centre of the city. The building was a square, flat-faced affair, put up early in this century, and it gave the impression that there had been no lack of money going into its construction, but a considerable lack of imagination. Victorian libraries always seem to start from the assumption that reading is a very, very serious affair. To get myself in the mood for an interview with Tetterfield I got past the desk and relaxed by having a leisurely look around. The heaviness of the outside was matched by the interior. The shelves were weighty monstrosities, built to last several lifetimes, and they stretched so high as to involve masses of little stools and ladders, which stood around in the open spaces asking to be tripped over. Much of the research material consisted of leather-bound books in long series, which didn't lighten the atmosphere: the reader felt he was in a Victorian Archbishop's study, surrounded by Crockfords for the last century and a half, or volumes of the duller sort of evangelical sermon. I'd never felt like a Trollope character before. A dreadfully heavy place it was, and yet one could imagine, festering here, the madder sort of collector's passion.

As I stood browsing around the shelves, pretending to be interested in the stately brown tomes, a little man came out of a back room, and bustled fussily over to the two young ladies at the desk. He was about fifty-five or sixty, scruffily dressed in what once had been good clothes, but loaded with cocksureness and self-importance. He wagged a finger as he gave some message or other to the young ladies, and then trotted back inside, clearly pleased with himself. The young ladies were rather drear pieces of respectability, but as his door shut one of them almost imperceptibly raised both eyebrows and shoulders to the other, and then returned to the business of filing cards.

I let them get on with it for a few minutes, because they looked like the kind of young lady who likes to get on with things. Then I replaced on the shelf the volume of *Improving Addresses* by the Revd Canon Theodore Price Merrivale (privately printed in Huddersfield in 1843) and strolled over to the desk.

'I wonder if I might speak to Mr Tetterfield?'

'Dr Tetterfield? Oh—I'm afraid you're too late. He's just gone home.'

'Was that him I saw here a few minutes ago?'

'Yes. But he has his own private exit. Dr Tetterfield *always* leaves promptly at four-fifteen.'

'Then I wonder if you could give me his home address?'

She looked at me suspiciously.

'Are you selling anything?'

'Do I look like a vacuum-cleaner salesman?'

'A vacuum-cleaner salesman would find no use for his product at Dr Tetterfield's, I assure you. No, I thought you might be selling him literary material of some kind. And I can tell you, people who peddle that sort of stuff come in all shapes and sizes. And degrees of reliability.'

'Well, I'm not that either. I'm a policeman.'

'Oh—well, I suppose I'd better give you the address.

But I advise you: don't go around there before seven. Dr
Tetterfield has his nap immediately he gets home from
work. He is definitely not to be disturbed.'

'This is police business.'

The young lady sniffed.

'Someone who rides roughshod over the cataloguing
rules is not likely to pay much attention to the law of the
land. If you want anything out of him, I'd advise you to
wait until he has woken up. Otherwise his response is
likely to be tetchy.'

'Why not say bloody-minded and have done with it?'
drawled the other young lady, in impeccable Roedean
tones.

Well, I talked with them a bit about recent bringers of
literary material, but I got no joy out of that. If Miss
Wing had been to see Tetterfield, she certainly hadn't
done so at his place of work. Then I snuffled around the
books a bit longer, getting very bored with population
registers and Dictionaries of Yorkshire Worthies. Then,
when the pubs opened I had a pint in a deadly little
place, all varnish and stale beer, not far from the library.
At five past seven I was ringing the doorbell of Dr
Tetterfield's home, an imposing Victorian three-storey
and basement job, set in its own half acre of ground. A
man with a bit of money of his own, the people at
Milltown had said. I could believe it. There was a long
wait on the step, but eventually the door was opened by a
massive woman in an apron, arms akimbo, eyes
suspiciously peering, exuding all the charm of an East
German female discus-thrower.

'Yes?'

I had decided to play it unofficial for the moment.

'I'd like to see Dr Tetterfield. Could you give him my
name, please? It's Peregrine Trethowan.'

She looked at me as much as to say 'A likely story!' but
what she actually said was a grudging, 'I'll see.'

Whereupon she shut the door in my face while she went to do so. This time, though, the wait was not long. She returned, shaking her head dubiously, and said: 'He'll see you.'

When I got into the hall, I saw why she had shut the door. The place was littered with books, manuscripts and typescripts, as well as tea-chests full of what looked like old clothes and other memorabilia of the Yorkshire great.

'Mind your feet!' snapped my charming guide. 'This stuff's valuable, so they tell me!'

We picked our way up the stairs, in semi-darkness, and little bundles of this and that, tied with string and labelled, adorned every step of the way. The landing turned out to be as littered as the hall, and we hopped from empty space to empty space, like hikers crossing a swollen torrent on stepping stones. Finally she opened a door and we came into a brightly lit study, similarly encumbered with the literary junk of centuries, but made more welcoming by a splendid large desk, and by walls of books that gave the place colour and warmth. Seated in a little armchair by the empty grate was Dr Tetterfield.

'Ah!' he said, advancing and rubbing his hands.

Dr Tetterfield, seen from close to, was not as unprepossessing as might have been guessed from the distant prospect of him, or the words of his assistants. He was small, but spry, and his eyes had a beady, bird-like sharpness. On the other hand, his voice was high, a strangulated treble, and his clothes seemed to have been bundled round him by some kindly Salvation Army lass—they bore traces, too, of egg, stew and other culinary experiences. And his welcome seemed to consist of little chuckles and snuffles, expressive of a delight in seeing me that was well beyond my deserts.

'Ah—Mr Trethowan. I don't have to guess who you are. One of the Northumberland Trethowans, eh? Fine family—it's an honour to make your acquaintance.

Sherry, my boy?' He took from a bookcase in the corner two perfectly beautiful cut-glass sherry glasses, shone to sparkling perfection, and a matching decanter. The place was altogether the oddest mixture of luxury and squalor I had come across.

'Always think it's better to sip at something while one does business, eh?' he snuffled.

'Er—'

'Is it Mr Lawrence Trethowan's manuscripts you're offering? Recently dead, I believe? A loss to letters, but it was a long and fruitful life—that's a consolation for you, I'm sure. Not precisely a *Yorkshire* writer, but still—we can stretch a point, eh?—stretch a point.'

As he came over with the sherry, I became aware that the housekeeper was still in the room, standing by the door, her arms folded over her intimidating bosom, and looking like the sort of prison wardress who is going to consign Susan Hayward to the gas chamber in the last reel. Dr Tetterfield saw my glance.

'Ah—er—you may go, Mrs Hawby.'

The housekeeper sniffed. 'You know how these people put it over you. I'll not have you done down, like you usually are. I'll stay.'

'I can put your mind at rest,' I said. 'I've nothing for sale. I've no idea where my Uncle Lawrence's manuscripts are, and they certainly wouldn't be mine to sell.'

Dr Tetterfield was in the act of putting the glass into my hand. He seemed to be within an ace of snatching it back.

'Disappointing,' he said, as if I had deceived him. 'Most disappointing. There now, Mrs Hawby, you can go.'

'I think I'll stay, all the same,' she intoned massively.

Dr Tetterfield looked uncertain, but he motioned me to an armchair, and as I sank into it whispered hopefully:

'She goes off duty at eight.'

Well—we were a cosy little gathering. I felt like an

aristocrat in the Bastille, being watched over by Madame Defarge. I sipped my sherry, to give me confidence.

'Nevertheless,' I said, 'I am on business, and it does concern a manuscript.'

'Ah!' said Dr Tetterfield, brightening up at once, rubbing his hands and emitting those high squeaks of anticipation that suggested nothing so much as a tiny rodent in the claws of a cat. 'Ah!'

'The manuscript is one you may have seen, or one which may be brought to you. It may be—it has the appearance of being—by one of the Brontë sisters.'

In the scruffy, disorganized body in the next chair I sensed an immediate access of tension. There was a short pause, and when he spoke he showed none of the interest or excitement which in such a collector would have been the natural response.

'I know of no such manuscript,' he said. 'No specific one, at least. And who, may I ask, do you represent in this matter?'

'I represent the CID,' I said.

'You silly old bugger,' said the housekeeper from the door. 'You've gone and got yourself mixed up with the police.'

He looked daggers at her.

'There, there, Mrs Hawby. You don't understand. He-he-he—*women*, Inspector, eh? Eh? Now, what was it precisely you wanted to consult me about?'

One thing I could not do, at that moment, was accuse him. Or even insinuate any connection. And yet there was something about him, some indefinable air, that made me want to. As it was, I could only circle vaguely round the subject.

'Well, now,' I said, 'I gather that nobody has come along to you with an offer of any such manuscript?'

'No, no. Would they had, eh? A real find that would be. No, I'm afraid not, Inspector.'

He was more relaxed now, and in his greater ease he seemed to give off a distinct air of hugging himself—of being delighted with his own cleverness or good fortune, or of enjoying some little private joke very much indeed.

'I suppose you get to know a great deal about literary manuscripts that may be up for sale?'

'Tolerably much, Inspector. I have the resources of the library, and a limited private source of funds. People have got to know this.'

'You buy both for the library and for yourself?'

'In effect the two are indivisible. I have no heirs. On my death my collection—modest, but I like to think not entirely contemptible—will go to the library.' There was a snort here from the direction of the door. Either Mrs Hawby did indeed think the collection contemptible, or she could think of other destinations for her employer's money.

'I see. And there is library money too?'

'Precisely. Under the terms of Josiah Brunskill's will—doesn't he sound like a character from a Thomas Armstrong novel?—we have an income from investment that amounts to some twenty thousand a year. Not riches, but it has proved most useful. The specific purpose is to buy manuscripts or other memorabilia connected with local writers and artists.'

'An enlightened man. So people—members of the public—come along with things of possible interest?'

'Quite. Or I contact them. Sometimes they're too modest to realize that what they have is of value. There are writers who never imagine what interest might be attached some day to, for example, their old clothes. But they soon catch on, they soon catch on! Sometimes I go along to their funerals. Find out the next of kin. Sometimes I do a bit of detective work on my own, and come up with things. This pen, Inspector—' he brandished a perfectly ordinary fountain-pen which had been lying on his desk—'this pen was the very one used by Phyllis Bentley to write her great novel *Inheritance*!'

I left a suitably respectful pause.

'Then you don't know the name of Miss Edith Wing?'

He looked at me sideways, then puckered his brow in thought.

'I can't say I do. The Wing family was once notable in—where was it?—the Halifax area, I think. But I can't say I recollect this particular name.'

'And nobody else has been along to you recently, offering a long manuscript in a handwriting that resembled the Brontës'?'

'No, no indeed, Inspector.' There erupted from him at that moment something that seemed to be a high-pitched chuckle. He made haste to cover it up. 'The only time I have been offered any manuscript by one of the sisters it was a letter from Charlotte, written in her later years, accepting a dinner invitation from the Wheelwright family. Hardly a prize item, yet it was snapped up by the University of Texas at a price well beyond what we could afford. A bitter pill, to lose our artistic heritage in that manner, eh, Inspector? It *is* Inspector, isn't it?'

'Superintendent,' I said. 'Well, I suppose there's nothing further to ask you. Obviously, if you *do* get offered any such thing, we'd be glad if you'd contact us.' I got up. 'Express interest, but contact us as soon as you can.'

He rubbed his hands delightedly, and seemed to be suppressing great wheezes of self-congratulatory laughter.

'I will of course, Inspector. Superintendent. Naturally. And, Superintendent—'

'Yes?'

'If there *should* be any question of selling family manuscripts or other things—'

'I'll put the seller straight on to you. I should like the thought of my Uncle Lawrence's hearing aid joining

Phyllis Bentley's pen.'

I made my way out, preceded by Mrs Hawby, who trod across the cluttered landing and down the stairs with all the delicacy of a Soviet tank entering Kabul. She was not, I suspected, in a good humour. At the door I turned to her.

'Was he telling the truth?'

'As far as I know.' She shrugged her massive shoulders — it was like a tidal wave in the South Atlantic. 'You can never tell with him. Childish, you know. Like all these what they call intellectuals.'

And she shut the door in my face. As I made my way down the overgrown pathway I reflected that, in its way, this interview had been as odd as the one I'd had with Timothy Scott-Windlesham. Not only had Tetterfield expressed no interest or enthusiasm when the subject of the Brontë manuscript first came up, but he had never subsequently asked about the nature of it, or its likely authenticity.

As I opened the gate, I thought I saw, some way down the tree-lined road, a figure slipping from the shade of a tree into a front garden. It was just a movement, in the corner of my eye, but it bothered me. Because the shape — I could make out no more — seemed vaguely familiar. I paused and watched. I thought I caught the sound of two voices, talking in a low tone. But after waiting a minute or two I shrugged and got into my car.

It was not until next morning that I heard that during the night Dr Tetterfield's house had been ransacked, and he himself tied up and subjected to prolonged mistreatment that almost amounted to torture. I thought then, again, about the shape under the trees.

CHAPTER 8

THE RICH ARE DIFFERENT FROM US

The devil of it was, the silly old bugger refused to talk. He just lay back there in the hospital bed, three-quarters dead, and insisted that he didn't know the men who'd done him over, didn't know who they were working for, and didn't know what they were after. It was this last thing that gave him away: it was impossible to believe. We kept asking him what the hell he was tortured for, if they didn't tell him what they were trying to get hold of, but he just answered that he supposed they were kinky, that they were just ordinary thieves, after his valuable collection, and so on. He produced this word 'kinky' with a self-satisfied smile, as if it was highly ingenious and explained everything. I suppose I ought to have admired the obstinate old lunatic in a way: it took guts, when you'd been worked over with fists, razors and God knows what else, to lie back there writhing in pain and still produce that air of suppressed self-satisfaction. Me, I just cursed my luck, in that as usual I had got myself involved in a case where half the cast list seemed already three parts along the road to the psychiatrist's couch and the padded cell. In the end a self-important young doctor bustled along and forbade further questioning, and I didn't quarrel with him. I could see there was no point in going over the same ground yet again: old Tetterfield was going to hug to himself the details of what had happened to him, and why.

After I left the hospital I called round to his house, where Mrs Hawby was proving more than a match for six or seven stalwart Bradford cops. My God! It was chaos in there — Winifred Holtby's bras all mixed up with J.B. Priestley's pipes, the pleasant study reduced to a wreck. A search of a random, frenzied, indiscriminate kind had obviously taken place, proceeding parallel, no doubt, to the treatment of poor old Tetterfield. The question was, whether anything had been found. I extricated myself as quickly as possible from the ruins, bearing as best I could the baleful looks of Mrs Hawby, who for some obscure reason seemed to hold me directly responsible for the affair. I drove thoughtfully back to Miss Wing's cottage. I despatched Constable Bradley down to the Dalesman for a lunch-time snack, and as luck would have it, that was when Jan rang.

'I suppose Nanny is in the room, making sure you don't say a word out of line?' she began nastily.

'As it happens, no.' I was very frosty.

'Right — fill me in on every detail. Quick, while he's away,' she commanded. And of course I did what I was told.

'Hmmm,' she said, when I had finished. 'The plot thickens. In fact, it's got distinctly lumpy, don't you feel, Perry? You got the impression that both Windlesham and Tetterfield knew where the manuscript was, did you?'

'Well, yes,' I said cautiously. 'But it was only an impression.'

'That seems to be one too many, doesn't it? They can't both have stolen it.'

'No reason why not. Certainly they could both be involved.' I had my own ideas about that, but I didn't go into them. Jan is much too prone to take on a Girl Friday role in my cases, quite unasked. 'Whatever the truth is, old Tetterfield seems to have paid the price.'

'And yet he's still not talking.'

'No. And of course he has every reason not to, if he's been involved in the theft of something as valuable as this manuscript could turn out to be. Stiff gaol sentence — end

of career. But I don't think it's just that: in fact, I don't
think it's that at all. You should see the way he's *hugging*
himself still. Either he thinks they didn't get it — he could
have passed out before they did. Or else he's hoping to get
it back again.'

'He knows who the thugs are, you mean? Or who
they're working for? You know, Perry, when you think
about it, don't hired thugs seem awfully unlikely?'

'Sweet innocent little thing. Hired thugs have been a lot
commoner than nice little old ladies these twenty years
and more. And unemployment doesn't diminish the
number. You can live in London and doubt the existence
of hired bully boys?'

'No, of course not. But *here*. I mean, in this sort of
case. Lost work of literature, and all that. It's so out of
character. I can believe in unscrupulous academics and
cracked librarians in this connection, but hired thugs — ?'

'Perhaps,' I admitted, 'it is a bit out of keeping. But
don't forget that appalling cousin. He's lived and worked
in Los Angeles, remember — "there *is* sin, there *is*
shame" ' — I imitated his ghastly nasal pulpit pomposity.
'If there's any sin or shame going, I bet the Reverend
Amos Macklehose is in there shamelessly sinning.'

'That's a point. But he seemed to think it was still in the
cottage, didn't he? Perry — have you seen today's papers?'

'Heavens, no. No time for that. You surely don't want
to talk about the latest Gallup ratings of the Social
Democrats, do you, Jan? I'm busy, you know.'

'Don't be potty. *Or* pompous. It's just that in the
Yorkshire Record there's mention of a millionaire — an
American multi-millionaire, a well-known collector. And
he's currently in Bradford.'

'*Really?*'

'What on earth would he be doing in Bradford, Perry?'

'Buying the Town Hall, I would hope,' I said. But I was
definitely interested. Bradford was not a Mecca for multi-

millionaire æsthetes — if that, indeed, was what the gentleman was, and not just a grabber. I could be interested in a grabber.

'Any details on what he collects?' I asked.

'They mention pictures — he's got several Samuel Palmers already in his collection — and a "fine Turner", they say. But *also* manuscripts of the Romantic poets.'

'Hmmm. Not spot on, but it could be worth following up. What's his name?'

'James L. Parfitt.'

'Fine old English name. Probably spoils it by adding "the third", or something. Well, thanks, Jan — I must go. I can hear Bradley coming back.

'Don't let Nanny find out you've been a naughty boy,' said Jan.

She can be a bit aggravating at times.

Bradley and I had a snack of tomato and cheese sandwiches, and ale that tasted of the can. I rang up Scotland Yard and asked them to get on to the States and see if the FBI had anything on James L. Parfitt. While we were jawing and gobbling Bradley, with a heavy flourish, produced a piece of news.

'Know who the old girl left her money to?'

'Who — Miss Wing? No.'

'Jason Curle. The little blackie.'

I didn't like Bradley's racial attitudes, but I met them often enough day by day to ignore them.

'We haven't a chance of getting at her will,' I said. 'How do you know?'

'That's what they say in the village,' he said, with his dull obstinacy.

'That's what who says in the village? People say all sorts of things in villages in my experience, and only about twenty-five per cent is anything like truth.'

'Everybody's saying so. I think it was Mrs Hebden as let it out. Her as was Miss Wing's friend around here.'

'No reason why she shouldn't leave it to him, anyway,' I said.

'Nor why she should, if you ask me. Wasn't any relation—just came in to do the garden.' Getting no change out of me, he just looked ahead with that bullish expression on his unintelligent policeman's face (I mean, of course, his unintelligent-policeman's face), and said: 'I just think it's funny.'

He sounded like the Reverend Macklehose's pearl of great price. If Jason Curle wasn't careful he would find himself the possessor of a tidy little fortune, with everyone for miles around muttering 'I just think it's funny,' and looking at him with gallows in their eyes.

I said: 'The woman hasn't got any relatives, her best friend was the one who left her all this stuff. She just likes the boy, that's all.'

'It's a motive.'

'If he knew. I bet she didn't tell him. She's too sensible to give him ideas that could only unsettle him. And she could so easily change her mind. Anyway, can you see that sort of injury being inflicted by a thirteen-year-old?'

'None of the blows was especially hard,' said Bradley. If he *did* get an idea into his head, no power on earth was going to get it out again. 'And he's pretty spry.'

'You'd need to be more than spry,' I answered, with comparable obstinacy. But I wasn't as sure as I sounded. You can't be dogmatic about injuries like that. I bet no one thought Lizzie Borden could wield an axe to such good effect.

I chewed over this, and the conversation I'd had with Jan, and I came to two decisions: one, to go to Bradford; two, to drop in on the way on Mrs Hebden. When she opened her front door to me her aspect was very different from what it had been when we were looking for a room. She was, not to put too fine a point on it, flurried.

'Oh—Mr Trethowan. Oh dear, I thought you might

call. I feel so guilty. You've heard—?'

'My constable just told me. Is it true you let something slip about Miss Wing's will?'

'Oh, the will. Oh dear—I'm afraid I did. Awful of me, but you see Miss Wing did tell me, just after she'd made it. That she was leaving the cottage to little Jason, and a bit of money too. Of course she swore me to secrecy, but somehow with the attack . . . and fearing she would not be coming back . . . I really *am* sorry. The last thing I'd want would be to cause trouble.'

'Nothing to be done,' I said. 'I think it might help, since it is round the village, if you made it clear to everyone that Jason Curle knew nothing about it.'

'Oh, you don't mean they're saying—?'

'If Constable Bradley is anything to go by,' I said, turning to go, 'that is *precisely* what they are saying.'

I chewed over this as I drove back to Bradford, and I chewed over the American millionaire I had decided to go and see. I'd bought the *Yorkshire Record*, but it had little more information in it than Jan had already conveyed, though one did get the distinct impression that the man was rolling in it. And, as a consequence, a very natural person for the thief to get in contact with, assuming that what the thief was after was money. The Yard wasn't much help, though. I had a message over the car radio that the FBI had no sort of file on James L. Parfitt—quite the reverse: the only time he had swum into their ken was when he had come forward voluntarily, when he suspected he might have come into possession of stolen property. Quite the lily-white boy. I told the Yard to cable for all possible details on this episode. I don't trust lily-white boys, when they're millionaires.

Still, I had nothing to go on, as far as Mr Parfitt was concerned. (How incredibly drab that sounds, for an American multi-millionaire: why don't they follow the logic of their society and introduce titles?) He was a collector, he was in Bradford. Now I came to think about it, away from Jan's eager insistence, it didn't sound ridiculous at all. The North Country has plenty of old family homes, full of old family pictures, old family silver, and old family debts. In economic times like the present there were even more upper-crust gents than usual pathetically in need of the ready. I had no grounds at all for connecting him with the Brontë manuscript. Nor was I enamoured of the figure much loved in fiction of the rich collector who stores up hot property to gloat over it in some private hideaway. Most millionaires like their treasures to be on display. Very much on display, in most cases, to reinforce their millionairedom, so to speak.

On the other hand . . . The Brontë manuscript was not all that hot. If Miss Wing were to die, or never regained consciousness, there would be practically no one around who could identify it with any certainty. I could not, that was for sure, from my brief glance at one page. In two or three years the manuscript could be produced, with a fictitious pedigree . . .

I consulted the AA Book for the two or three best hotels in Bradford, pretty sure that James L. Parfitt would not put up at an overnight joint for commercial travellers. By luck I hit on the right one first time. It was called the Royal Edward, and for once it lived up to its name. The foyer was all white and gold and plush pink, with spotty mirrors in gilt frames; scattered around were pink and gold velvet sofas, on which one could imagine Royal Edward perching his ample frame, perhaps placing his hand on a not-unwilling knee the while, or pinching a be-bustled bottom while whispering an assignation. Through the door to the left I caught a glimpse of an oak-panelled dining-room, where one could imagine him eating one of his piggish meals. It was all rather daunting—as if I'd strayed on to the set of one of those BBC historical serials for television. I mustered what courage I possessed and strolled up to the desk.

'Er — Mr James Parfitt.'

'Oh yes,' said the spruce young picture of efficiency behind the desk, to my surprise. 'Just take the lift — there —' he pointed to the far corner of the foyer — 'up to the third floor.'

I had a feeling I'd been mistaken for somebody else, but not wishing to kick my luck I simply did as I was told. As soon as I emerged from the deep padded silence of the lift I realized I was right. I seemed to have barged in on the early stages of some kind of party. Mr James L. Parfitt had apparently taken over the whole of the third floor of this wing of the hotel. The great wide corridor, hung with prints of dogs and horses and jockeys, was peopled with maids and flunkies, and as I stepped out, more than a little embarrassed, a pretty little thing dressed in apron and starched cap came up with a sweet smile and a drinks tray. This time I felt as if I'd walked into *Upstairs, Downstairs*.

'Whisky, sir? Or sherry? This is dry.'

'Yes, I'll have a sherry. Er —'

'Mr Parfitt is through the doorway there, sir, at the moment. I'm sure he'd like you to introduce yourself. It's the sitting-room of the Rose Suite.'

I gulped, and went in the direction she pointed. The sitting-room of the Rose Suite (which was *very* rose) was beginning to get rather crowded, and being both an impostor and an intruder I hung back by the door until I could be sure which of the well-dressed drink-clutchers was Moneybags Parfitt.

It was quite a collection of people he'd got together there: an immense lady with a voice like a foghorn who had obviously tied her horse to a parking meter and was wondering whether its time was running out; a North Yorkshire Duke with a minor post in the government and a stately home twice the size of Sandringham; an Earl with property in West Yorkshire who had sold the land on which the University of Milltown was built — a gaunt, joyless individual who was reputed to smile only when he went over the estate books which dealt with that transaction; various scions of the local squirearchy — portly, doggy, genial, rather awkward; and a squad of local business smoothies trying to look as if brass had not the remotest connection with muck.

'Hello, thinking of selling the family pictures?' said a voice from beside me.

'They're not mine to sell,' I said automatically, and then looked round to see a man in his forties — gentryish, friendly, with a nondescript face and a sardonic downward turn to his mouth.

'Well, I can't see your getting much for your old dad's manuscripts,' he went on, digging further into my sore spot.

'Have we met?' I asked, in a dowagerly way.

'Long, long ago. You were just out of short pants. Witteringham's the name. Frank Witteringham. Frightful name, what? With most people you forget the name and remember the face. With me it's the other way round.'

I remembered, dimly, Frank Witteringham, and shook him by the hand. His people had property near the Co. Durham border of Northumberland, twenty miles or so from Harpenden.

'Of course,' he went on, with that sublime ignorance of tact so characteristic of his type, 'I didn't really remember you. I just recognized you from your pictures in the paper.'

'Yes,' I muttered, internally wriggling.

'What are you hoping to get out of this gravy-train, eh?'

'Nothing,' I said. 'Are most people?'

'Of course they are. Why do you think they're here at two or three days' notice? Look at that chap — Duke of

Hull. Oh, you recognized him. Should be in the Lords, speaking on the new Rates Act. He's junior minister, after all. 'Stead of which, he's here. Got something to sell, smells a good buyer. That's why we're all here—what?'

'Really?' I said. 'And how did you all know? Were you invited?'

'Not in so many words. It went round on the grapevine. He'd been snuffling round at Christoby's, and the other big places, and he let it be known that he'd be in Bradford, happy to see anyone with anything of interest—etcetera, etcetera. Jolly good network most of us have. I heard it from my kid brother who works in the City, and he heard it from a chap who works on Debrett, who heard it from a chap who's one of the buyers for Christoby's. So Bob's your uncle, here I am.'

'What have you got to sell?'

'Hmmm. Highly dubious Reynolds, and a bit of family silver. He won't bite, and I wouldn't blame him. Still, I thought I'd pop along. Look at them—they're streaming in. We'd better get a bit closer if we're going to have a word.'

And so they were—or at least, they were coming in a steady trickle, with alternately brazen and slightly embarrassed airs. All grades and styles of gentry and near-misses were there, and coming on for twenty-five in the room already. I followed my guide, and as we began edging our way to what was obviously the focus of attention, Frank Witteringham muttered:

'What *are* you selling, then?'

'Nothing.'

'What the hell are you here for, then?'

'Official. I want a word with him.'

'Oh, great. That'll put him in a splendid mood, won't it? I'm going first, young Trethowan.'

And it seemed only right I should let him. Particularly as I wanted to get a good look first. I stood by, watching

Frank Witteringham do his piece, and taking in the set-up. It all looked so casual and spontaneous. There was James L. Parfitt, standing there, glass in hand, all geniality, as if he were an ordinary man like the rest of us. He was dressed in a superb light-weight suit, and a sober tie; his hair was highlighted silver, and his tan was coffee-cream and even all over. He was tall, distinguished, with the remains of handsomeness about him, and a supremely confident and relaxed manner. But there was also something unreal, as if he were an actor, already made-up, and beginning his performance.

He listened to Frank Witteringham like a Renaissance prince lending an interested and concerned ear to the tale of a loyal peasant. As the meagre extent of Frank's offering became clear, I caught his eye shifting from him and wandering round the room, but only when he knew Frank was not looking. In no time Frank was passed on to a young man standing casually near—a dark-suited, bespectacled young man, no doubt a secretary, rather resembling those young men in the Watergate saga who were always telling you about their Methodist upbringing, and how they and their wives went down on their knees each night and prayed on either side of the matrimonial bed. He took Frank's name with an appearance of interest, and then he was handed on to say hello to Mrs Parfitt, who had collected a little group of prime notables around her. He said hello, but he was not collected, and he then drifted off into the outer darkness. By then I was myself talking to the Great Man, and feeling as if I'd barged into a Neil Simon play.

'I'm afraid I'm here under false pretences,' I opened. 'I wanted to have a couple of words with you, and I was sent up by the receptionist under the impression I was one of the guests.'

'No harm done, no harm done,' said James L., with limitless geniality. But I registered that his eyes were beginning to stray. 'Was it something we could get through fairly quickly?'

'By all means,' I said. 'I'm from Scotland Yard—'

'Scotland Yard! Well! This is an event! You'll have to have a word with my wife. She's mad about your English detective stories.' He suddenly lowered his voice. 'But, say now, I hope there's nothing wrong with anyone *here*?'

'No, no,' I said hastily, to dispel the idea of a spectre at the feast. Nothing but upper-class sharks here. 'No reason to think that at all. It's just that—well, some publicity has been given to your presence here, as a collector . . . I wonder, by the way, why you came to the North of England?'

'Well, there's no mystery about that.' He lowered his voice, though. 'Just keep it under your hat. I'd heard that the big houses in the North were great untapped sources of the sort of thing I'm after. And the people not so—well, so grasping as those down South. Not so in touch with the market.'

Mugs, he meant. I felt like saying I wouldn't bank on it.

'Ah—I see. What I wanted to ask was whether you've been offered, while you've been here, a manuscript—'

'Several, naturally—'

'By the Brontës. By one of the Brontë sisters.'

He didn't bat an eyelid. But I noticed that his eyes had stopped straying too.

'Regretfully no. Nothing so interesting, as yet. Mind you, there's a mountain of that stuff around in the States. Mostly bought years ago, and a lot of it finding its way into libraries by now.'

'You haven't got any Brontë material yourself?'

'Nothing to speak of, Inspector. It's a big collection, you understand, and I don't have it all in my head . . . There's a poem by Emily Brontë, I remember, bought by my father, back in the 'twenties, I'd guess. Oh, and one of those little childish books. I guess that's about it.'

'You haven't been interested in that sort of stuff yourself?'

'I'm interested in everything, Mr Trethowan. But especially interested? Well, no. My father had a nice little collection of manuscripts that I inherited, and when I came to enlarge it, I decided to go for the Romantics. I guess you can say I went for the best. But that's certainly not to say I wouldn't be interested . . .'

'But you've had no offer of that kind to date?'

'No, sir.'

'We'd be most obliged to you if you'd get in touch with us if you should be approached—either the Yard, or the local police.'

'Indeed I will. I'm very careful about that kind of thing, as the New York police will testify, if you get on to them. But tell me, Mr Trethowan, you've raised my interest now, and you'll have to appease it—what is the precise nature of this manuscript? I'll need to know, won't I, in case I'm offered it. Is it one of the juvenile manuscripts?'

I went carefully. 'I think not, though it looks very like them. It's a work of prose . . . It could be a novel, or part of a novel . . .'

He whistled. 'You mean a mature work, then. Wow! That would be something big.'

'Well, I won't take up any more of your time, Mr Parfitt—'

'Do you have any more details, I mean—'

'Let's just say, sir, that we'd be glad to be told if you hear of *anything* in that line.'

'Cagey, Inspector. Well, I surely will have you informed.' He smiled a cool but friendly smile. As I was shunted forward to the secretary I noticed an almost imperceptible shake of the head from Parfitt, caught by the secretary's sharp little eyes. He shook my hand with excessive bonhomie, but he did not take my name. As I was handed down the conveyor belt to Mrs Parfitt, her husband called out:

'You must talk to Mr Trethowan, darling. He's one of your Scotland Yard detectives.'

'Oh *really*?' said Mrs Parfitt, turning aside from one Duke, one Countess, and a couple of knights of the shire. 'How fascinating! I can see you *must* be. Just my idea of Roderick Alleyn!'

I thought Roderick Alleyn a bit of a stick. I became stick-like.

'Are *all* the policemen at Scotland Yard gentlemen of the old school, like they are in detective stories?' asked Mrs Parfitt. She obviously read an old-fashioned sort of detective story, but everything else about her was bang up-to-date. She was twenty years younger than her husband: a highly desirable thirty-five, with immaculate hair, immaculately made-up face, immaculate figure, but with a touch of steel-plating about it.

'Not all of us,' I answered. 'Most of us even have a bit of trouble with our French, like Fox.'

'Oh, you read them, then!' She turned on one of those special for-you-alone smiles that Americans are so good at. 'I thought you'd be sure to despise them. And what are you doing here— are you checking up on His Grace?' She smiled in the direction of the Duke of Hull.

'No, indeed. I'm actually checking up on a missing Brontë manuscript.'

'Really? And could my husband help you?'

'Not as yet, anyway. You haven't heard of it?'

'Oh no. Where manuscripts are concerned I'm a dimwit. I couldn't tell one of those dreary sisters from the other. Furniture is my thing— my very special passion in life.' She turned a fraction of an inch back towards the Duke, who must surely have been well-furnished. '*So* pleased to have met you, Mr Trethowan.' She had remembered my name, with that miraculous transatlantic faculty for such things. The smile, though, was one of super-cordial dismissal. I slipped out of the charmed circle.

Back by the door I took a deep breath. All that suaveness, and well-oiled charm, and money, took it out of one. However did they keep it up? I took a whisky from a passing tweeny, who smiled and sketched a curtsey. I decided she must be a recent graduate of drama school, unemployed. The local toffs were still wandering in, nervous but hopeful smiles engraved on their well-bred, under-chinned faces. I looked at them as if it were an identity parade, and they swerved off in the other direction. However, Frank Witteringham wandered along to where I stood, holding two whiskies.

'So that I can say my journey was not entirely wasted,' he explained.

'No luck?'

'The nicest possible cold shoulder. Why would he be interested in a dubious Reynolds of one of my ancestors? There's the Duke with a Poussin, some of the best Chippendale in the country, and a Hilliard miniature—all discreetly on offer. Did you get what you came for?'

'No,' I said. 'I don't think I did.'

I downed my whisky, made fond farewells to Mr Witteringham, most likely never to meet for another twenty years, and went out into the corridor. No, I didn't think I had got what I had come for. I ignored the lift and started off thoughtfully down the stairs. If James L. Parfitt was a crook, he was a good deal better at it than the bumbling amateurs I had met hitherto. One had the sense of dealing with class, in that as in every other respect. There had not been a flicker when I mentioned my profession or my business. He had expressed a healthy and natural interest in the nature of the manuscript. Of course, one had the impression throughout of an incredibly quiet machine, performing its functions. Mrs Parfitt had even managed 'His Grace'. But it would be in the nature of things that the whole operation would be smooth. American millionaires must run a very neat ship. No, there was no reason at all to suspect Mr James L. Parfitt.

It was as I descended the last flight, down into the pink plush of the foyer, that something happened. I was aware, out of the corner of my eye, of two figures entering the swing door of the hotel. They turned naturally in the direction of my staircase, but as they caught sight of me descending they did the smoothest of about turns and marched straight out into the street again. No doubt they were sure I hadn't seen them. I hardly had. But I recognized their shapes, and the backs of their heads. They were the two men I had seen coming out of Timothy Windlesham's office.

CHAPTER 9

EAVESDROPPING

I could have run after them, of course, and tried to catch them up. But what could I have said to them if I had? Instead, I nipped over to the foyer window of the Royal Edward, and watched them walking through the car park outside, down to the street. They were going at a fast lick, straight ahead, almost marching, and by their size intimidating other casual walkers out of their way. At one point the taller of the two swung his head round purposefully and looked towards the hotel entrance. Satisfied, he swung it back, and kept on striding ahead. I watched them till I saw them swerve left towards Bridge

Street, then I streaked after them.

I kept well behind them, but my eyesight is good and I managed easily to keep them in view. They went down Bridge Street, past the Town Hall, then up Sunbridge Road. It's a straight hill, which helped me keep them in view. Once, again, the tall, fair one swung his head round to look behind him, but I was in a doorway inspecting the lower shelf of a display of ladies' slippers by the time he had focused on the street. I was pretty sure he had not seen me. On they went, now much more relaxed. They came to an intersection with a phone-box, and the taller went in while the other remained loitering outside. I became fascinated by what Bradford's Stereo Centre had to offer. After a minute he came out, looking puzzled and bad-tempered. He shook his head at his companion, and muttered something. Then they were off again. They plunged into that bewildering maze of hilly side-streets I'd driven around before. Left, right, left, up, down, into a shopping centre, into a market. Real thorough boys, these. Finally they turned into a large pub with a long frontage and a dimly-lit interior.

I lingered outside, peering through the mottled glass, but I could see nothing. I didn't want to go in before I was sure they had got their drinks and were perhaps settled down at a table. But mightn't they be watching the door for new arrivals? I noticed a tiny alley down one side of the pub, leading to a notice that said Saloon Bar. I nipped down and pushed the door open, and found myself in the sort of bar that only the furtive or the incurably respectable would patronize.

There was a door into the Public, and I found I had an excellent view of it. The two were leaning—looming, almost, they were so large—over the bar, and being served with pint mugs of—not beer, it seemed, but perhaps draught lager. I watched them try it, then wander away from the bar into the body of the cheerless,

wooded, high-ceilinged barn of a room. There were
tables and benches in rows in the body of the place, and
frosted glass panelling between them, making some
attempt to produce a more intimate atmosphere. The
men went away from me, and I saw them take seats on
opposite sides of a table on the far side of a glass panel.
I paid for my beer, an extra 2p or so, then to the
barmaid's surprise I dodged through the door into the
Public and strolled nonchalantly over to the table on the
other side of the glass panel. The fair heads were
unmistakable. I put my pint down on the table, and slid
into the bench.

At first, with the buzz of conversation around me, I
found it difficult to tune my ears in to their talk. There
were people at the nearby tables — talking about dog-
racing, pigeons, the government, and all sorts of
nonsense. Then I caught their tones — very low for two
such large men, and blurred. I could hear them talking,
but I could not hear what they were talking about. I
edged along the bench, closer but not too close to the
frosted glass. They obviously had no suspicions. They
were leant forward over their table, their heads close
together. As they got deeper and deeper into their
conversation their voices got higher and higher in tone. I
could hear what they said, but —

They were talking in a foreign language.

I sat there kicking myself and cursing my luck. I should
have thought of that. Just the look of the men — two fair
men together, big, well-built, not an ounce of fat on
them. It wasn't English, somehow. I sighed, and tried
once again to tune my ears in.

It wasn't French — that, in spite of my remarks to Mrs
Parfitt, I could have managed. Nor, from the sound of it,
was it any of the Mediterranean languages. They looked
about as Latin, anyway, as Ingrid Bergman in *For Whom*

the Bell Tolls. German, then? No, it didn't have the guttural heaviness of German. Scandinavian, of course: one or other of the Scandinavian languages. Just what one might have thought, looking at them.

Which didn't help much. Knowledge of the Scandinavian languages is not widely diffused, and it certainly wasn't diffused in my direction. I tried to make out individual words. Now and again something popped up that I thought I understood. 'Leeds', surely? But who could say whether 'Leeds' meant anything in Swedish, or whatever it was. Then I heard a name, twice. Waddington. Only he said it with something between a V and a W at the beginning. Who was Waddington? Their boss? I *thought* I heard the word 'manuscript', or something like it, but I couldn't be sure, it was all so fast and low. I felt like a blind man at a strip show. If only I'd got a cassette recorder, I could have taken it to a linguist later. I sat there, fuming, and hoping that perhaps the name 'Brontë' would occur.

But when a name came, it wasn't that. 'Tennyson'. I heard it as clearly as anything. A minute or two later, it came again: Tennyson. What the hell had the Old Queen's tame bard to do with all this? What connection was there between Tennyson and Emily Brontë? Those two particular misty mountains never came together, surely? There it was again! You'd think they were bloody research scholars. I sat there in mounting frustration.

Then I sensed movement in the booth beside me. Were they going? Would they go back and make another attempt on the Royal Edward? But no: they took their glasses. They were going to the bar again. With blessed prescience the architect had placed a long mirror behind the counter, above the bottles. By turning sideways I could study them out of the corner of my eye as they stood there waiting for their refills.

The taller of the two was the one I had got the best

sight of so far. Thickset, in good trim, with cream-coloured hair and regular features, but with something of heaviness about him that was not a heaviness of body only. Now I got a good look at the other one, and he could never in a hundred years be English — but, oddly enough, nor did he look particularly Scandinavian either. His hair had a silvery fairness, it is true, but his face had a lowering, almost Mongolian impassivity about it: blank, massive, cruel. That was the impression of the body too: he was shorter than the other one, but even wider — a tough, threatening muscularity. I didn't like the look of them at all. They looked, as Jan said, like thugs. They looked like somebody's heavies. I was so fascinated I tipped my drink over as I turned to get a better look. I swung back round and retrieved most of it. Then I crouched over it for a minute or two.

When I looked back they were staring unsmiling ahead as their drinks were brought. The tall one slapped down a couple of pound notes. When they turned round from the bar I was slumped low over my beer again. How long would they stay? Where would they go when they left? I waited for them to sit down. And waited. Surely they wouldn't be likely to stop and chat to anyone. They hadn't the air of pigeon fanciers, or of being at home in this kind of place at all. I cranked my head round cautiously, but I couldn't see them. Still they didn't come. I turned round more openly, anxious. Then I got up and scanned the whole barn of a Public Bar.

They must have rumbled me when I upset my beer. They were nowhere to be seen.

And of course when I went to the door on to the street there was no sign of them there either. At an empty table in the middle of the bar there were two full pint mugs of draught lager. They had obviously spotted me in the mirror, registered nothing — they had the kind of faces built for registering nothing—and then when they had got their beers they had set them down and scarpered. I had bungled the whole thing.

Not that I would have been likely to get much out of any further overheard conversation. Eavesdropping on a foreign conversation is a bit like observing the sex life of earwigs—a lot's going on, but you don't get the point of it at all. But I might have followed them again, perhaps found out where they were staying. I somehow couldn't see them going back to the Royal Edward now, not after they'd seen me there, then spotted me listening in to their conversation—even if they could have been pretty sure I would not have understood it. I finished my beer, feeling frustrated and fed up with myself, and went out into the street.

What does one do in Bradford on a drizzly summer evening? The various options didn't seem enticing: the streets were nearly empty, but there was the odd window-shopper, the odd street-corner punk, and I supposed there might be the odd multi-cinema, where I could go and see one film and hear three. I toyed with the thought of an Indian meal, but my stomach said 'Not on your life'.

Ringing up Jan didn't seem likely to restore my self-respect, but I'm a bit of a masochist, so I rang her up just the same.

'Jan,' I said, when we'd made our greetings, 'did you bring all those books on the Brontës up to Harpenden with you?'

'Most of them. All except the ones that were totally and absolutely ga-ga. Why?'

I told her the whole story.

'Well, you didn't distinguish yourself, did you?' she commented brutally. 'A right fumble-bum. Do you know, men got demoted in the Victorian force for less than that?'

'Stop wallowing in nostalgia. I'm not looking to distinguish myself on this case, just to get hold of that manuscript.'

'You don't seem to be making much of a hand of that either.'

'You do do marvels for a man when he's down, Jan. Now, will you go and look up those books? I want to know what connection there was between the Brontës and Tennyson.'

'Oh — hell, Perry, they're in the Georgian wing. Ring me back in ten minutes, will you?'

Harpenden is the sort of house that makes you wish escalators and moving walkways had been invented a little earlier. I rang off, and spent the time ringing the West Yorkshire Metropolitan Police at Leeds, asking them to contact all the hotels and guest-houses in the Leeds and Bradford area, to see if any of them had had a couple of Scandinavians staying there. They said it might take a bit of time. Bradford has never caught on as a holiday resort, but there were scores of small places for commercial travellers. I told them to get on to it. Then I rang back to Harpenden. Jan answered the phone, breathless.

'Give me a chance,' she said. 'Do you realize how long it takes to get around this great barn of a place?'

'I should do. I was brought up there. Now you'll start to appreciate the flat in Maida Vale.'

'Well, I do begin to,' she admitted. 'My ankles are beginning to swell. Wait a minute, I'll look in the indexes.' There was silence, except for the sound of pages being flicked over. 'Well, really, there hardly seems to be any connection at all. Emily liked Tennyson's poems. Charlotte and Anne brought her back a volume when they went to London . . . A few references here and there, but that's about it.'

'There *must* be more to it than that,' I said. 'Or

perhaps there isn't any real connection: perhaps they were talking about something else—some other manuscript altogether.'

'*Two* manuscripts, with the heavies after both?' queried Jan. 'It doesn't sound very likely. Too wholesale altogether.'

'You're right there,' I admitted. 'Then why this mention—three times I heard it—of Tennyson?'

'Perry—will you be at the cottage tomorrow?'

'I suppose so—if you catch me early. Why?'

'Oh, nothing. Just in case I wanted to ring you.'

And she rang off, leaving me as dissatisfied as when I had rung her, and a mite suspicious as well. What did that last bit mean? Had Jan got an idea, one that she was holding out on me with? It seemed only too likely.

There was nobody outside waiting for the phone. There was nobody outside at all. Bradford in the rain really is *not* an enlivening place. I decided on a little experiment. I heaved up the local telephone directory, found the number of the Royal Edward, and rang them.

'Could I speak to Mr Waddington, please?'

'One moment, and I'll see if he's in,' said the receptionist. They never call you 'sir' if you ring from a phone-box. After a moment I heard 'I'm putting you through', and then 'Hello-o-o,' in an American accent and a (or did I imagine it?) slightly wary voice.

'Oh, good evening, Mr Waddington. My name is Trethowan. We met earlier. I just wanted to apologize for gate-crashing Mr Parfitt's party this afternoon.'

'Good heavens, no apologies needed. He was delighted . . .'

'I feel bad about it. I certainly wouldn't have gone up if I'd known. But you will keep in mind my request to let us know if you get any offers of Brontë material, won't you?'

'Surely, surely. I've made a note of that already. But nothing so far, I'm afraid, Mr Trethowan. And that's a real shame, because it sure would have been nice to pick up a Brontë item in Brontë country, wouldn't it?'

It sure would have, Mr Waddington, I thought, saying my adieux and ringing off. And I wasn't at all sure they hadn't managed it already.

CHAPTER 10

AT THE SIGN OF THE RISEN MOSES

After a night spent tossing and turning in one of Miss Wing's inadequate little beds I arose next morning with sore bones, a general feeling of depression, and a sinking sense that I had little or no idea what to do next. Which way was my decidedly erratic investigation going to direct itself now? Admittedly there were some loose ends to be cleared up, and I pottered around clearing them—phoning here and there to fill in the picture. I checked with the hospital and there was a glimmer of good news about Miss Wing's condition: there seemed to be signs of returning consciousness, though they were still unsure how far the brain was affected, and it would certainly be several days before she could be questioned. Then I heard from the Bradford police about two Scandinavians who had stayed at an obscure guest-house on the outskirts of the town. They had checked out yesterday, with no forwarding address. They had given their names as Hans Olsen and Jens Nilsen, of Oslo. Ho-ho, I thought. The Norwegian equivalent of John Smith and Bill Brown of London. Another door slammed in my face.

For there really did not seem to be anything very obvious to follow up next, and I could hardly sit around in the cottage day after day at the Yorkshire police's expense, waiting for something to turn up.

It was at that point that Jan rang.

'Hello. Still feeling down in the dumps?'

'I'm certainly not dancing tiptoe through the clouds. So if you've rung me up to tell me what a cock-up I'm making of this case, Jan, you can just ring off. I have no idea where the manuscript is. The two Scands have disappeared, leaving behind them nothing but false names and Oslo as their address. And I haven't had a single idea about any possible connection Tennyson may have with the case . . .'

'Ah yes, Tennyson,' said Jan, with an unmistakable ooze of self-satisfaction in her voice. 'I rather think you may have been barking up the wrong tree there, Perry.'

'You mean not Alfred, Lord?'

'No, more Björn Borg.'

'I beg your pardon?'

'I've been on the phone to a friend doing Scandinavian languages at Newcastle.'

'You all do the oddest things at Newcastle. But go on.'

'In Norwegian the definite article "en" is added to the end of masculine nouns . . .'

It took quite some time to sink in.

'Oh, Christ. Tennis-en. You mean the blighters were just talking about bloody tennis. Well, thank you very much, Jan. That's another door up another alley closed in my face.'

'Do you really think so, Perry? Surely they wouldn't have been talking about going to play a genteel match or two as a break from the serious business of thuggery? You said they looked as if they were talking business. Perry, I don't know if you've seen the papers today—'

Then I cottoned on.

'Of course! I've been seeing posters all over. The North of England Championships. Opening at Leeds—when was it?'

'Saturday, Perry. Tomorrow.'

'You're a wonder, Jan. Take back all I've said hitherto. You are a bloody marvel. Every policeman should have one.'

'Quite. Of course, there may be nothing in it at all.'

' "When a burglar isn't occupied in burgling, he loves to play at tennis in the sun"? No, Jan, you're quite right: it's business they were talking about, the business in hand, not their regulation one day off in six, or keeping fit. In any case, I couldn't chance it. I've got to be there. I suppose your mention of Björn Borg doesn't imply he will actually be playing?'

'Good heavens, no. Nor the one with menstrual problems either. It's just a peanuts-plus sort of show. But the current British champion will be there, and dozens of British has-beens, so there'll be plenty of people going.'

'Probably that's the idea. But at least I will be there too. And I don't suppose I'd have been able to see Borg anyway. I'll keep in touch, Jan. I mean it—I really will.'

'You'd better, boyo.'

I rang off, feeling quite irrationally delighted. Something to do, a lead to follow, a possibility of gold at the end of the rainbow. I'd never actually thought of Leeds as the end of the rainbow, but I was quite willing to start doing so. I certainly was hitting the hot-spots of the North on this case. When I saw Bradley pottering up the garden path to come on duty for the morning I decided to go to Leeds at once. It would be worth wasting a few hours, to get my bearings in the city. That had its dangers, of course: if the two Scands saw me, they would probably call the whole thing off, whatever the whole thing was. Still, I decided to risk it.

So I drove there feeling unusually light-hearted, and booked into a modest hotel, which was nearly empty for the weekend, all the usual commercial gentlemen having taken themselves and a new store of excruciating jokes home to their ever-lovings for the weekend. I went along to the brick fortress of the West Yorkshire Metropolitan Police, and set them on to making further enquiries for the two Norwegians, now presumably centred on Leeds rather than Bradford. It seemed a genial enough force, and I was made welcome. They promised to do what they could, discreetly. I had a bite to eat in the hotel dining-room, and regretted it. Then I took to the streets of Leeds.

What I would really like to have done was to disguise myself. It sounds terribly corny and Sherlock Holmes, and I don't suppose I would ever have convinced anybody as a cab-driver or a match-seller, but I would have felt a lot better observing the place from behind some impenetrable get-up. The Authorities do not rule out absolutely extravagant behaviour of that kind, but they are very inclined to ridicule it. But the decisive count against it was the fact that at six feet five and seventeen stone I'm a hell of a difficult object to disguise.

So I went as I was, but I didn't feel easy, and I kept being sure that I was being observed by my quarry, but was failing to spot them. I went to a few obvious pubs, a few obvious chain stores, but mostly I just walked. I changed my mind about Leeds. Briggate and the streets around are a bit depressing, apart from the arcades, but once off them Leeds was rather a handsome city, or the ruins of one. These days you need X-ray eyes to see what it's been like, or a very good historical imagination, but that's true of most big cities. I liked the way they built confidently, massively, in those days. The Town Hall tells you they knew Leeds was the centre of the universe. These days we build massively but not confidently—hence places like Milltown.

But you could see the days of confidence and unlimited brass were gone. Puddly car-parks, cut-price shops and decayed warehouses abounded. It depressed me rather.

Medieval cities in decay are wonderful and moving, but industrial cities in decay . . .? I think I must be a romantic at heart. I got off the main streets and began wandering around the less prosperous residential areas, the side-streets and bye-alleys, with their smells of chips and uncollected garbage, their air of in-grown dirt and depression. The evening sun was watery, but warm and pleasant, and a slight haze gave soft outlines to the shabby buildings. There were few people about, and as I wandered I almost forgot what I was there for. Until, that is, my attention was suddenly arrested by a sign:

TABERNACLE OF THE RISEN MOSES

and underneath:

CONGREGATION OF THE NEW ISRAELITES

It was a squat, square building, a brick box, devoid of any ornament. Very likely it had once belonged to one of the minor subdivisions of English evangelical Protestantism, and had been built in early or mid-Victorian times, when theological passions ran high, and schisms could occur over the interpretation of *Isaiah* ch.VI, v. 14. Over the years, no doubt, the congregations had dwindled, seduced into agnosticism or bingo, or become worshippers at one of the more socially accept-able venues. Until now, when it had fallen into the hands of — yes —

PASTOR: The Revd Amos Macklehose, MA, D.Div.

Soapy Amos himself, with his dubious creed, his dubious morals, and his doctorate to match. I peered closer:

MAIN SERVICE: Sabbath Gathering, Fridays, 8 p.m.

So, they celebrated the Jewish Sabbath. How very convenient for me. It was now half past seven, and there was a little pub opposite. I slipped into it, ordered myself a double vodka (that fond belief that no one can smell if you've been drinking vodka!) and stationed myself by the window. The pub was nearly empty, and the landlord behind the bar seemed a taciturn bloke, but I tried him out.

'Many people go to that church place over the road?'

'Oh, aye,' he said, with that air of forcing words out, a few at a time. 'Fair few . . . Pretty rum place, from what I've heard . . . Ah, there's nowt queer as folks.'

Well, I'd never expected to hear that last bit outside the pages of one of the novelists Dr Tetterfield collected relics of. By the time I was finished savouring the experience the landlord had pottered off, no doubt glad to rid himself of the nuisance of a talkative customer. I turned back to the scene outside.

By dribs and drabs the congregation started turning up. One or two married couples, but most of them on their own. Women predominated slightly, but no more than in a more orthodox religious assembly. There were hardly any children—children assert their rights these days—but there were a few young people, mostly on their own. There was something about most of the congregation: something drab. Perhaps a lot of unemployed went there, to keep warm, to relieve the monotony of existence. I could imagine Amos Macklehose relieving the monotony of one's existence. There was something . . . what was it? . . . slightly furtive about many of them, too. As if they were satisfying a craving for something hardly reputable, were tapping an illicit brew, and were nervous of the excise men. They clutched their dreary fawn or grey coats around them and scuttled inside, looking neither to left nor right.

I didn't think most of them would be my kind of people.

All in all, though, I calculated the Reverend Amos had attracted between fifty and sixty hearers that early summer's night. Not bad. It was a tribute to the skills learned on the wilder fringes of Californian religious life. At two minutes to eight I downed the last of my vodka and slipped over the road. I had to resist the impulse to clutch my raincoat around me and scurry in, head bent. But when I got in, I slipped into a seat in the back row, shady and anonymous.

I say shady, but none of the church was well lit, which added to the feeling of furtive pleasures, illicitly indulged in. Only the—what shall I call it?—the stage, the altar, was bathed in a flood of light. A long table was draped in a startling scarlet cloth, which had a flash of yellow lightning running across it. On the top was an enormous gold or gilt cup, such as one might imagine figuring in an amateur pageant about the quest for the holy grail. There was, of course, no stained glass, but on the wall at the back was painted an enormous sun, gilded and flickering, against an inky background.

All very theatrical. But for the rest it was must, and damp, and shadow, and we all sat in our little privacies, waiting for the show to begin.

I slumped forward, chin down, trying to get a glimpse of the worshippers around me. Sitting by the door, doom-laden and unapproachable, sat Amos Macklehose's pearl of great price. She was staring ahead of her, in the manner of the self-righteous, and I could not tell if she had seen me. Immediately in front of me was a little bald man with National Health spectacles and a dirty fawn mac, looking like a plumber in a small way. Near him there was a dim woman under a large felt hat with an aggressive feather on it, wearing an old, dun-coloured coat and clutching a large brown hold-all that looked as if she was intending to spend the weekend here. There was a thin adolescent boy with lank fair hair and spectacular pimples, ripening nicely. There was a prim piece of respectability in a beige cardigan, her mouth formed into a moue of distaste, her hair wound round the back of her head in a plait. Beyond stretched more of the same kind—the same drear colours, the same inhibited solitariness, the same prissy expressions. It looked less like a religious gathering in the nineteen-eighties than a Fabian Society discussion group in the eighteen-nineties. Except that, about this group there was a tiny spark of tension, of expectation. As if they knew something worth having was going to be vouchsafed them, that they would indeed sip the mountain dew drawn from the illicit still. I expect you got the same sort of feeling in the audiences that went to Elvis Presley concerts in his last years.

'Have you scrutinized yourselves today?' came suddenly a voice from nowhere.

At that moment the few lights in the body of the hall were switched off, doubtless by Mother at the back. Here and there a timid voice answered: 'Yes. Yes.'

'Have you? Have you searched into your souls? Ransacked every nook and cranny? Have you got down on your hands and knees and done a real spring clean of the spirit?'

Every moment the voice seemed to be coming dramatically nearer. Then suddenly there flashed a new, more brilliant spotlight on the altar, and a fantastic figure darted to the centre of the stage.

'Have you? Because unless you have scrubbed for the Lord, unless you have swept for the Lord, dusted and scoured for the Lord, your place is not here.'

He gazed round them, seeming to look into their eyes.

'No, my friends, your place is not in the House of Moses. "Go, for thou art unclean in my sight," as the Lord said to Ezra. "Hide thy shame, for the House of the

Lord knowest thou not," as He spake to Potiphar. Our Lord's not one for an off-white soul, oh no. He'll know whether you have sluiced yourselves out. Have you? Have you shone the spotlight into the darkness of your souls?'

'Yes!' said the voices, more confidently now. 'Yes! Yes!'

The Reverend Amos Macklehose looked around his congregation, with earnest, searching interest. His former shiny, grubby black had been transmuted into a splendid purple robe, flowing from his neck, and hiding his paunchy, buttocky figure. On the chest of the robe there was a brilliant gold sun, with angular beams spreading from it, echoing the sun on the wall behind him. He looked large, theatrical, yet not quite the impressive figure he was obviously aiming at. Above the sparkling sun on his chest one saw the sparkling eyes in his greedy, cunning face, as it eagerly surveyed the forms of his congregation, his milch cows.

'And what did you find there? Did you find a clean, well-lighted place?'

'No — no!'

'Or did you find a grubby, dusty, dark cellar of the spirit? Did you find a black hole? Did you find a gaping, yawning gulf of sin?'

'Yes! Yes!'

'That's what we find when we spring clean, isn't it? And that's what we find when we get round the U-bends of our souls. Dirt. Grubbiness. Darkness. We find the secret sins we've hidden from everyone else, don't we? We find the sins we've even hidden from ourselves. Lying there. And *festering*. Festering like a piece of meat in the summer's sun. Festering like an old wound, untreated. Spreading infection throughout the land. WHAT DID YOU FIND?'

There was a tense moment for thought. Then suddenly:

'I found lust!' shouted the boy in front with the spectacular pimples (and I wasn't at all surprised). He stood up: 'I found unclean thoughts about women.'

'Have you cleansed yourself?'

'Yes. No!'

'Cleanse yourself now! Sing Hallelujah! Praise Moses the prophet! Shout: Moses saves!'

'Hallelujah! Moses saves!'

'I found greed!' suddenly sang out the mousey woman in front with the spiky feather and the capacious bag. 'I looked into my heart and I found lust for gold!'

'Cleanse yourself!' roared Amos, with more than usual enthusiasm. 'Sing Hallelujah!'

'Hallelujah!'

'Give to the work of the Tabernacle! Give to the spreading of the word! Give to proclaim the Risen Moses! Spread the Commandments! You will get a chance soon—'

Imperceptibly he gestured with his head to the back of the hall, and turning I saw two large, fleshy young men, heavy but out of condition, who had taken the place of the pearl beyond price, and who were standing, dark-suited and lowering, by the door. They held plates, and it looked as if it was going to be more than my life was worth to try to get out without coughing up.

'Come to me,' crooned Moses, gazing at the mousey woman. 'Come to me privately, Sister Boothroyd, if your soul is troubled.'

'I found covetousness,' shouted an elderly man from the front of the hall, a busybody type who obviously felt that no meeting could be considered complete without his dreary testimony. There were plenty who felt the same. We went through the usual round of sins, which I need hardly spell out for you, as well as one or two I hadn't thought of. Would you ever have imagined that complaining about the government was a sin? Yet here was this silly old biddy getting to her feet and shouting:

'I have grumbled in my heart against the Lord's

appointed rulers of this land!'

I found it hard to think of God controlling British elections with some divine swingometer in the sky, even with Bob Mackenzie up there to help him. Even Amos Macklehose gave her rather short shrift. But for the most part he kept things going with unfailing zest, and every now and then when Testimony flagged he would come back fighting with:

'Are you ransacking the corners of your hearts? Are you seeking out the twisty byways of the soul?'

And after the Testimonies he would proclaim 'Moses lives!' or 'Hallelujah, Brother, you are clean!' Or sometimes:

'Come and unburden your soul to me privately, if the spirit fails you now, if the sin gnaws too deep!'

This last bit interested me. I tried to work out some pattern to his saying it. Was it just to the sisters he said that? No, it wasn't. Was it just to the sins with financial overtones that he said it? No—he wasn't that stupid. But perhaps it was *mostly* to the sins with financial overtones. Or was it sins that he thought he might *use*?

Like all these things, the public shriving generated its own momentum, but then gradually died away. Before it expired into a whimper, the Reverend Amos got a grip of things:

'Do you feel cleaner, brothers?'

'Yes! Yes!'

'Do you feel whiter than white, sisters?'

'Yes! Oh yes!'

'Then we will now, before the Address, have a collection. Give to proclaim the Word, brothers! Give to spread the great joy, sisters! Give to testify to Moses Risen, Moses present among us, here today. And remember, brothers, sisters. Remember: I am your stay, your support, your staff, your foundation. If you should feel the need for personal Testimony, if the spirit should move you to bare your soul in private, come to me, your support, your foundation. Come to me on Tuesdays or Thursdays. Come to me, all ye who are heavy laden, and ye shall find rest!'

And as the Reverend Amos slid over into rank blasphemy, a movement at the back of the hall signalled the start of the collection. I was in a bit of a quandry. My first impulse was to tear a button from my blazer, fling it into the plate, and leave. On the other hand, I did not want to make myself conspicuous by crossing the flabby pair of youths who I felt sure were the offspring of Amos and his pearl in a sow's ear. The thought of staying to the end, however, was quite intolerable. I had by now a fair idea of Amos Macklehose's speaking style: it was Mr Chadband out of Aimée Semple Macpherson, and I couldn't face a whole Address in the same vein. And if I stayed to the end, what if Amos imitated the Established Church and stood at the door to shake our hands? I felt I would hardly be able to resist kneeing him in the groin. As the plates approached me I saw they were beginning to fill with notes. Cursing myself for cowardice and the Bank of England for abolishing the ten shilling note, I drew a crumpled pound from my pocket and threw it in. Then, as the young men, unsmiling, advanced further down the hall, I slipped round the back of the last row of chairs and escaped into the night.

The fresh air smelt good, and I hurried down to the gate. But, having a sudden thought, I turned back to look at the notice-board I had seen originally from the road. Close to, I could read the details. There it was. Services Friday night and Sunday morning. Personal Testimony: Tuesdays and Thursdays, from 10 to 12 at 25 Pankhurst Road.

What a very unpleasant idea. Private confession, without any of the safeguards of the confessional. Unpleasant, and how very dangerous too, with a shepherd of sheep who was mainly interested in their fleeces. I wondered what precisely the Reverend Amos was up to, not merely in connection with the manuscript, but in his normal line of business. I decided to stick around for a bit, and went round the corner where a high brick wall shielded me from view from the church. I lit a cigarette, and heard that high voice with the suggestion of American accent ringing out his Address. I lingered round under the benign sky, but still the Address did not end. I had smoked three cigarettes before some movement was heard. A trickle of people began reluctantly to tear itself away from the preacher's fascinations. 'What I like, it's always that bit *different*,' I heard a woman say as she went through the gate. And from the door of the chapel I now heard his voice again.

'A great pleasure, Brother Hebblethwaite . . . Glad you enjoyed it, Sister Nichols . . . Yes, I felt the wind of inspiration blowing through me tonight, indeed I did, Brother Hooper . . . See you on Tuesday, then, Sister Boothroyd. It will do you good, I know it will.'

And then, when all the congregation had drifted away, cleansed, I heard the voice, in lower tones, say:

'Did you see that big guy at the back, boys? That's the cop I ran into at Hutton. Think you'll remember him again? Your mother pointed him out, did she? Both of you be very, very careful of that guy.'

And the voice of the minister of God faded into the night.

CHAPTER 11

DOUBLE FAULT

You couldn't quite say that all the world and his wife were going to Leeds for the tennis, but a lot of the North was, and they — and the sun — brightened up things considerably. The 'wife' part tended towards hats, floppy or flowery, and the 'world' part towards blazers and slacks, around and under paunches. Many of them seemed to know each other, and they lingered in the brick and stonedash streets of the Leeds suburb where the tournament was being held, hailing each other, exchanging small talk, and meeting up with others who puffed along from the point where they had been forced to leave their cars. There were lots of noisy kids, and generally the scene presented a Frith-like, bank-holiday atmosphere. Into which the Scandinavians, had they been there, would hardly have fitted.

But of course they were not there. Nor was it going to be easy to monitor their arrival. The Sports Centre where the tournament was to be held was, of course, a 'complex', and that about summed it up. There were four separate gates, and though I told the policeman on each of them to keep his eyes open for large, fair, foreign-looking men, two of them, possibly together — I was nevertheless not hopeful. For a start, if they had sense they would not come together, and singly they would be a lot less noticeable. Then, they seemed to dress in a standard international fashion, and you had to look closely before you saw without doubt that there was something about them that was not English. Like the blank, almost Mongolian face of one of them. I had tried to describe that to the various bobbies, but I gave up when I realized they all thought I meant mongoloid. And big men there were in plenty, among the spectators. As people drifted past me a daft fragment of conversation floated my way: 'I do like a man to have a bit of meat on him,' said a woman to her friend. Most of the men around seemed only too happy to oblige her.

It would have been easier if I had known what they were there for. Knowing that, I might have been able to guess where they would do it, or how, and make appropriate preparations. To justify my presence there at all I had to assume it had something to do with the manuscript. That certainly seemed a reasonable assumption, in view of their turning up both in Timothy Scott-Windlesham's office and at James L. Parfitt's hotel. Not to mention their visitation on Tetterfield, because I felt morally certain that it was the shape of one of them I had briefly glimpsed in the street outside, and quite certain it was they who had done the poor old silly over.

The tennis must surely have been selected because it was the big event in the current Leeds calendar: that is, whatever was to be done, had to be done where there were thousands of people milling around, to give cover. It seemed to me likely that this was done on the orders of James L. Parfitt, or more specifically on those of Mr Secretary Waddington. The one who had made the phone call had been given the rounds of the kitchen for trying to see him at his hotel, because the gilt-edged boys were dead scared lest their connection with the manuscript be traced. In future, nothing but phone calls, and above all a maximum of obfuscation of the scent. So the next step had to be undertaken in a place guaranteed to cause maximum confusion — for fear that the Vikings were being followed.

But what was the next step?

One thing I was willing to bet: they had the

manuscript. I was made the more certain of this by something I'd heard that morning. Dr Tetterfield had been released, at his insistence, from the hospital, and a Bradford policeman had gone along to drive him home, and to make a last attempt to frighten him out of his complacent silence. But the complacent silence had been undented, and had been mingled—the chap said—with a sort of excited anticipation. After he had delivered him home, and had swapped heavy incivilities with his mountainous housekeeper, he had lingered in the doorway, warned by some sixth sense. A few moments later he had heard a despairing wail, and the voice of Tetterfield calling for his housekeeper. This made it pretty clear: after he had passed out under treatment, the Vikings had found what they were after, and had stolen it.

And now, presumably, they were passing it on. But to whom? Certainly neither Parfitt nor Waddington would take the risk. They were the clean-hand boys, and likely to remain so, certainly for as long as they were in this country. One possibility was that they had decided that the Nordic duo had outlived their usefulness, and that the prize was to be handed on to another contact—one that would take it out of the country, perhaps. Take it over to the States, where in a few years it would surface, and no one would know for sure whether it was that dubious manuscript, which few had seen, which had been mentioned in connection with a certain murderous attack in a Yorkshire village . . .

That seemed a possibility, but there were other possibilities as well. There might be further processes the gilt-edged boys wanted gone through before they committed themselves to the ultimate risk of smuggling it into the US. They could, for example, want it verified by an expert. Risky. But there were plenty of crooked experts around. Or they could want to get a typescript made of it.

And then I saw him. The taller, Nordic-looking one. I was in the biggest open space in the Sports Centre, behind the courts, with gates away to my right and to my left. The crowds were milling, because the first matches were about to start, and some were going to one court, some to another. And there among them was the regular-featured, clear-eyed, slightly anonymous-looking man I was after, advancing towards me. I withdrew to the shadow presented by a sweets and ice-cream stall, and watched.

He was alone. He pretended for a bit to be going with one of the streams towards Court One, but he went slowly, and I could see his eyes were darting around, searching for something, someone. Who? Me? His menacing-looking chum? Surely not — he was looking, I now realized, *down*. And looking, though he was being very canny about it, mainly at the women. Being very unobtrusive about it, as I say, but in my job you get to acquire a certain expertise in people's aims and intentions. Like you know the chap sauntering through Soho, looking everywhere, seeming to be interested in everyone and everything, is really only interested in one thing, and if you follow him you can easily find out what. Well, this chap was interested in a woman — perhaps someone he knew, perhaps someone he had a description of. Coming towards the entrance to Court One, he seemed to be afflicted by a change of mind: he stopped, turned, and started mingling with the crowd going towards the other courts. He would pass close to the sweets stall. I sank further into the shadow and looked about me.

You certainly saw all sorts there. I'd always been a bit prejudiced about tennis — thought it a snooty sport, all strawberries and cream and the Duchess of Kent. And, to be sure, there was no lack of snoots around. I saw two of the people who had been fawning on the Parfitts in the hotel suite in Bradford: they were done up to the nines, and hail-fellowing it all over the show. I kept my eyes on *them* all right. But there were also coppers I'd met at the Leeds Police HQ—out with their wives and families, and presumably not on plain-clothes duty. There was a waitress who'd brought my breakfast that morning, and a member of Amos Macklehose's congregation (who presumably had wrestled with her spirit and decided that tennis too could be regarded as one of the gifts of God). So with the kids racing about the place and making a din, and the candy-floss and ice-cream being licked, the open areas round the courts had a real bank-holiday feel to them—much more so, I'd guess, than you'd find at Wimbledon.

The blond man strolled by me, deceptively casual, and I slipped behind the stall till he'd gone by. When I re-emerged he was still going in the same direction, towards Court Four, but as I watched he almost imperceptibly increased his speed. I darted from cover and went after him. He began edging out of the stream of spectators, and suddenly I saw coming from the other direction, menacing and unfestive in that crowd, his friend and ally. Almost without a glance at each other they met up, and—still without a sign—changed course and started towards the nearest exit.

I made a frantic gesture to one of the constables I'd talked to earlier, a sign over the heads of the crowd. I pointed towards the duo, and as he edged over towards the exit I came in behind them to shut off their retreat. They saw the constable, sensed something was up, and the blond, Nordic one looked behind him. He began to swerve aside, but then he seemed to have second thoughts: weight for weight he and his pal matched me and the constable. But with a hostile crowd they would have no chance. He put his hand on the arm of the other, and they continued walking until they came to a halt at the exit, their course stopped by a blank wall of constabular chest.

'Excuse me, sir—'

'Yes?'

'There's a gentleman here would like a word with you—a gentleman from Scotland Yard.'

The tall one turned, and looked at me—blond, neutral.

'Yes?'

His accent was neutral too. Like a lot of Scandinavians he could pass for an Englishman as long as he kept to monosyllables.

'I want to talk to you both,' I said, wasting no words. 'Is there an office?' I asked the constable.

'We've got a room in the administration building,' he said, nodding to the block behind us. 'I expect you could use that.'

'That'll do. Come along with us.'

'Is this necessary?' said the taller one, the spokesman. 'We are here for the tennis.'

'Are you? Odd you should have been making for the exit before the first game has begun, isn't it?'

He blinked. Fifteen-love to Perry Trethowan, I thought. We hove in on either side, and the four of us made our way silently to the administrative block. Once there I let the constable go, and we sat on either side of a bare deal table, looking each other up and down. The spokesman continued to look bland, totally cool, but the other seemed tense with bottled-up rage and a vindictive, indiscriminate violence.

'Your names?'

The big blond one paused, thought, and seemed to decide it would be foolish to go into the Norwegian version of the Jones and Brown routine.

'Rolf Tingvold. And this is Knut—' and then something quite unpronounceable.

'Do you have your passports?'

Pause again, then both of them took them from their pockets. Little red passports, Norwegian, the information inside typed. Rolf Tingvold, with an address in Hammerfest, North Norway. Knut Ratikainen, with an address in Vadsó. Several entry stamps indicating lengthy stays in the United States. Profession: seamen. They did not seem to have followed their profession for some time, but in the current state of the shipping business that was not unusual. I turned to the threatening, blank-faced one.

'Ratikainen—that's not a Norwegian name, is it?' I said to him. 'Are you a lapsed Lapp, or something?'

He glowered ahead, silent. It wasn't much of a joke, but he could have made the effort.

'It is a Finnish name,' said his friend. 'There is big community of Finnish descent in North Norway. He is born Norwegian.'

'I see. What are you doing in this country?'

'On holidays. Between jobs. We are seamen.'

'So I gather. And is Leeds the sort of place Norwegian seamen generally come to for a holiday?'

Tingvold remained neutral, unsmiling. 'Why not? We like to see the world.'

'Ah yes. And today?'

'We came to see the tennis.'

'Yet you were leaving before it even started.'

Pause.

'It was something to do. Before the pubs opened. But we change our minds, see? Because we was not specially interested. Tennis isn't so popular in Norway.'

'Difficult to play on skis, I suppose. So, having paid five pounds each, you leave without seeing a game.'

'No law against that, is there? We pay to come in, we leave when we want to. I tell you, we're not that interested.'

'Come off it,' I said, hotting up the pace. 'I saw you. You didn't *decide* to leave. You met up, and without a word you went to the exit. It was a prearranged plan. You'd done what you came here to do, hadn't you?'

'We decide to go. So who needs words? We know each other well, we don't have to speak.'

'Touching. I don't believe a word of it. What's your connection with James L. Parfitt?'

'Who? Who's he? I never heard of him.'

'I doubt that. What about Mr Waddington?'

'I don't know nobody with that name.'

'I saw you in Bradford coming out of their hotel.'

'So what? We go places to drink. Is that illegal?'

'I heard you mention the name Waddington in a pub there.'

'Ha. You understand Norwegian? You make a mistake, that's all.'

'I also saw you at Milltown, coming out of the room of Timothy Scott-Windlesham.'

'Where is Milltown? We never been there in our lives.'

'Stand up. I want to search you.'

That pause again—insolent, reflective, an assertion of latent power. From the Finn, sitting there, his silver fair hair glinting under the light from the ceiling, it was especially fearsome. But then they stood up. I went over them thoroughly. Wallets, pens, cigarettes—not a thing of interest. Ratikainen, as I searched him, seemed barely able to suppress a desire to tangle with me. His eyes thinned, his blank, asiatic face took on a look of infinite menace. His silence, his compliance, implied a storing up for the future.

I had an idea.

'Take your jackets off.'

They looked at me, with the usual powerful, threatening silence. Then they stripped off their jackets and threw them contemptuously over the table. They sat down again on their chairs, folding their arms, looking straight ahead of them.

I took up Ratikainen's jacket. It was a cheapish American job, stretched by his bulk, beginning to look tatty. I inspected the pockets and the linings. Nothing. Then I took up Rolf Tingvold's. Immediately I struck gold. Or at least solid silver. On the inside lining there was a long zip, carefully hand-sewn, with a sailor's skill. It ran almost from shoulder to waist. It opened to reveal a large, lined pocket, more than large enough to contain, say, a bulky foolscap envelope. It was empty.

'Unusual,' I said.

'Not so unusual. We are seamen. Is useful.'

'Funny I've never seen one before. And what was in it?'

'Nothing. We are in a hotel. All our stuff is in our room. We don't need to carry anything.'

'Oh no? Not a large envelope, for example? Containing perhaps a manuscript?'

'What is that, please? Manuscript.'

'Paper. With writing on it.'

'I don't write much.'

'You know perfectly well what I'm referring to. I'm referring to the manuscript you stole from Dr Tetterfield. Let me tell you what I think happened. You made an appointment with somebody, to meet them at the tennis. You wanted to hand on the manuscript in some crowded place, rather than going to their home, where you might be followed. You had a description of him or her, and perhaps a sign between you to ensure you got it right. And when you saw whoever it was, you passed the manuscript over, and immediately tried to get out. I, like a fool, didn't take you when I first saw you, when you still had the manuscript.'

'Is all a fairy tale.'

'And you brought little endearing here along with you, to back you up if there was any rough stuff.'

'There wasn't no rough stuff. We didn't make no trouble.'

'Not with two policemen. If it had been Mr Scott-Windlesham or Dr Tetterfield—that would have been a different matter.'

'Who are these people with the terrible names? We never heard of them.'

'Well, perhaps we'd better see about that.'

I collected a constable and a police car, piled them in, and we drove from Leeds to Bradford in silence. Or near silence, for they swapped a few muttered sentences in Norwegian. I thought they could have been contemplating making a break for it at traffic lights, so I kept my eyes on them all the way, but they brazened it out—sitting there in the back, solid, silent, apparently quite confident. And how right they were to be that.

At Bradford we drove directly to Dr Tetterfield's house. It was Saturday, but his housekeeper was on duty. The sight of her on one side of the door, guarding, and us four heavies on the other side, demanding admittance, was full of comic possibilities, but I wasn't in the mood for quiet humour, and the Scandinavian heavies looked as if their sense of humour had been deep-frozen at birth. After the usual wait we were led up once more to Tetterfield's study. He was sitting convalescent in his armchair, a pathetic sight, his face and hands dotted over with sticking plaster, a great blue bruise over his right eye. At the sight of the Finn he visibly flinched.

'Ah,' I said. 'You recognize these two?'

And quick as a flash the answer came back:

'No, no. I don't think I've had the pleasure.'

And the silly old buzzard started struggling to his feet as though we were making a social call. Why do I keep getting involved with raving lunatics in my cases? Other policemen spend their time with commonsense, down-to-earth, perfectly talk-to-able villains, yet as soon as there's a certifiable lunatic on the horizon, the case is neatly lobbed into my lap. Here was this frail elderly man, beaten practically unrecognizable, and yet he fails to point the most fluttering finger of accusation at his tormentors because he still nourishes hopes of getting his precious little manuscript back, of having it all to himself, of drooling and dribbling over it in the privacy of his home, among his assemblage of old socks and cast-off suspender-belts. I ask you! And when I saw the shoulders of my two thugs perceptibly relax, and something close to a smirk waft over the lips of Rolf Tingvold, I got really mad. I started shouting at the silly old goat, demanding that he recognize them, admit that they'd roughed him up, come down to the station and lay a charge against them. But if he had any fear, it was not of me, and he sat there, immovable, complacent, denying it all.

And so there I was, up against another brick wall. We all drove back to Leeds, and I put them through it at West Yorkshire Metropolitan Police HQ. By now they were visibly complacent. They—or rather Tingvold, who did all the talking—stuck to their story, which was really no story, a prolonged negative. They didn't know Parfitt, they didn't know Waddington, they didn't know Tetterfield, they didn't know Scott-Windlesham. If I thought I'd seen them coming out of Scott-Windlesham's office, then I must have made a mistake, mustn't I? Bang, bang went my head against the brick wall of their denials. The tables were turned since old Tetterfield's refusal to recognize them, and they had only to keep up their stone-walling and eventually I would be forced to give in. And in the end I had to admit it, and let them go. They got up from their chairs, silent, and marched to the door.

'Don't think you're getting away with this,' I said feebly, falling into cliché. 'I'll know you again.'

The Finn turned round, eyes narrowed, gazing intently, and spoke for the first time:

'And *we* shall know *you*, Mr Police,' he said.

CHAPTER 12

HOSPITAL VISITING

The next few days augmented a feeling I was beginning to have of my head being held firmly up against a brick wall. Little things came up, such as the first dribbles of information about the two Scandinavians from the US, but most of the stuff that was shoved in my direction by the police at Milltown, Bradford and Leeds illuminated little and led nowhere. I had long conversations on the phone with Jan, in which she was pretty scathing, but dismally failed herself to come up with any further suggestions of where the investigation might go next. 'Well, *you're* the one there on the spot,' she said resentfully, and with some truth. And I was on the spot in the other sense as well: I had a case to investigate, without the foggiest notion of the next steps to take; a manuscript to retrieve, without the first notion where it might be. Basically I was waiting till they allowed me to interview Miss Wing, without any great hopes of that getting me going again.

Meanwhile I went over and over in my mind the pattern of the case as it now presented itself to me. That the manuscript had been in the hands of Dr Tetterfield seemed to me incontrovertible—the only way I could account for his extraordinary behaviour. How it got to him was important for the attack on Miss Wing, though not so important for the ultimate destination of the manuscript. But the obvious connection between Miss

Wing and old Tetterfield was Timothy Scott-Windlesham, and I could easily see him committing the attack, in a frenzy of spite and fear. His motive in undertaking the theft was, I had no doubt, both academic and financial: he had no qualifications for editing a Brontë work, but if the manuscript could be kept under cover for a few years he could get himself qualified. And editing a newly discovered work by Emily Brontë would bring him academic kudos beyond his dreams. Not to mention an awful lot of money. Which no doubt was why he went in with mad old Tetterfield.

But then there was the question of how the real thugs, the professionals, came into the picture. Here things were much more misty, but I was ready to conjecture that the unsavoury old crook here (if he would pardon such an expression) was the unlovely Amos Macklehose. It was easy enough to see how he got wind of the manuscripts — either through a family tradition, or, more likely, through that cursed adherent of his in Hutton-le-Dales, who travelled regularly to the Tabernacle in Leeds, randy for robes and altar-cloths. Macklehose would certainly have been aware of the family's Brontë connection, and would have seen the plausibility of the story at once. From him to James L. Parfitt was a simple enough step, especially if Parfitt had just landed in the country and was already putting out feelers about his interest in buying. And Mr Parfitt had his strong-arm boys — kept at arm's length, probably never actually getting to see their patron. The thugs, I suspected, had come on a reconnaissance trip to Hutton, posing as Seventh Day Adventists or whatever it was, but they had left the action too late, and Timothy had popped in between intention and execution. They had followed the same trail as I did, and had had to catch up with the manuscript when it had passed to Tetterfield.

So far, so good. Then came that blank wall. They had

got instructions from Waddington, that I was willing to bet; and the instructions must have been to pass it on to someone. They organized the transfer at the tennis—crowded, chaotic, with very little likelihood of their being successfully prevented or properly observed. Clever of them, really. Because now I was back to square one. I had a list of four people who I was pretty sure had handled the manuscript at one time or another, yet I was no nearer to finding out where it was now. It had been handed on, and that was that. For all I knew the Norwegian toughs had now bowed out of the whole operation—leaving the field to heaven knows who. Mist had come down over the field of play, and for all one knew a whole new set of players were now kicking the ball.

As I say, I was far from confident that, when Miss Wing was well enough to talk to me, she would have anything to tell that would lead the chase more than a few steps further. But I waited, fumbled about with irrelevancies, and eventually on Thursday morning I got the message from the hospital in Milltown that I could go over and have a talk with her—but only for a short time.

It was a horrible glass and board sort of building, opened in the 'sixties but already looking as frayed and tatty as an ageing variety star. It wasn't the sort of place that Miss Wing fitted into naturally, but the staff seemed competent enough. The sister to whom I spoke, outside the room where she lay, stressed that the time at my disposal was limited, and she did it with the sort of emphasis that only sisters and matrons have at their command.

'She's a very sick woman still,' she said, 'and I shall rely on you in no way to upset her.'

She looked at me as if she had the strongest doubts whether she could rely on me at all. I was quelled, as men always are quelled by that sort of authority. I nodded meekly. She pursed her lips, said 'Well . . .' as if she would not be answerable for the consequences if I overstepped the mark, and led me into Miss Wing's room.

'Your visitor, Miss Wing,' she said, with surprising gentleness.

'Ah,' said the figure on the bed. 'They said I'd met you before. I wondered if it might be you.'

Ill she certainly was. Pale, bandaged, and still horribly scarred on the face. The voice too was faint, lacking that clipped, schoolmistressy precision which I had rather liked before. But there was still a faint spark in the eye, something about the set of the shoulders as she lay there, that made me think she hadn't given up, that in the end she would come back fighting and be as fit as she ever had been. I took a chair and sat down close by her bed.

'You tell me the moment you get tired,' I said. 'And just say "don't remember" if you don't—don't try and strain your memory. Close your eyes if it helps.'

'Oh—it's nice to see someone,' she said. 'I feel I've been half in and half out of life for weeks. Like being in a waiting-room at a station—between journeys, as it were. I'm not used to complete lack of mental activity, I can tell you. Ask away.'

'Well, now, you remember our conversation in the Dalesman?'

'Oh, very well. How is your charming wife?'

'She's fine. Now, I gather you did as I suggested, and went along to the University of Milltown?'

'That's right. A day or two later. A young man . . . I forget his name . . .' She put her hand to her head.

'Never mind. Timothy Scott-Windlesham it was. Now, do you remember what he said to you?'

'Well, he was perfectly kind, but . . . well, he didn't seem particularly impressed. I suppose he was right to be sceptical, but he seemed rather an—what we used to call an *effete* young man when I was a girl. I thought perhaps he didn't like to show himself impressed by anything. Languid, you know.'

'That may be the reason,' I said cautiously. 'Now, what did he suggest?'

'Well, he said he wasn't an expert, but he offered to keep it for a bit and look into it.'

'Did he indeed?'

'Yes. But I didn't like to let it out of my hands. So he said the best thing to do was to take it along to the big libraries at Leeds or Halifax, or somewhere like that. I said I had no car, but he said there was no hurry because usually these things turned out to be less exciting than one hoped.'

'I see. So you hadn't done anything more about it by the time you were attacked?'

'No, I hadn't. I think I'd found talking to Mr . . . whatever . . . rather depressing.'

'I see. When he was talking about libraries, did he mention the librarian of the West Riding Library, near Bradford?'

'I don't think so. No. I'm sure he didn't.'

'But you yourself had already mentioned the manuscript to people, hadn't you?'

She put her hand to her forehead again.

'Yes. You've no idea how foolish that makes me feel: a schoolmistress all my life, always cautious and practical, advising precautions against this and that. And then to go and talk about it in the Dalesman, of all places. And by the way, Mr Trethowan, I really ought to confess . . .'

'Confess?'

'Yes. I'd talked about the manuscript even before you turned up in Hutton. I told Mrs Hebden, who is a good friend of mine.'

'Ah — Mrs Hebden.'

'That's right. And you see, she recognized you. She knew you'd been involved in cases — of a literary nature.'

(What delicacy! Not a trace of the snicker usual when the matter of my father's murder came up. I really loved Miss Wing!) 'So you see, she rang me up as soon as you went down to the pub. And I — I feel awfully naughty about it — faked a casual meeting. I really don't usually go up and talk to complete strangers in public houses. Quite out of character, believe me. But I wanted expert advice, you see, and I felt sure you would be a good sort of person to go to.'

'Well, I wish, in the event, that I'd given better advice. And I'm very far from being an expert.'

'Well, much better than I could have got in Hutton, believe me. But I'm afraid that after that I mentioned the manuscript several times in the pub. All sorts of people could have heard of it. So foolish of me, as if I didn't know how any little thing gets around in a village like Hutton. I suppose that was the reason, really: so little happens there that when something does happen to you, you naturally want to talk about it.'

'I shouldn't reproach yourself. After all, when you took your manuscript along to an expert, you were bound to talk about it anyway, and ran the same risk of its getting around that you had it.'

'You mean the gentleman at Milltown? You surely don't think it could have been that, do you? I mean, a *professional* person . . . But I did wonder whether perhaps he wasn't as unimpressed as he made out . . . Well, I don't know. Certainly I should have told as few as possible, and I feel a silly old woman.'

'Tell me, do you think your cousin Amos Macklehose could have known of the manuscript? Perhaps by family tradition?'

'Cousin? Cousin? I don't count him as my cousin! How many removes do they have to be before you can consider them utterly removed?' Miss Wing's fighting spirit was very much in evidence at the mention of that name. 'All the same,' she went on, crinkling her forehead, 'I don't see how he could have known and not my cousin Rose—I'd consider *her* my cousin, however many removes there were! And I'm sure she didn't know. Because she was an English literature person, you see. A great reader, which I am *not*! And she would have been so excited if she had found it when she inherited the family papers that she would certainly have told me. If there had been any family tradition about it, *someone* would have investigated long ago. Because we've been going downhill for years!'

'That's rather what I thought,' I said. 'I mean about investigating, not about going downhill.'

She smiled rather frailly.

'He called, you know,' she said. 'That Amos creature. He was visiting one of his flock—a rather pathetic old man who finds the local church a bit too humdrum for him. Macklehose was visiting him, and he came to the cottage. But I wouldn't let him in. I'd had enough of him when Rose was dying.'

'Interesting,' I said. 'Now, let's come to the night you were attacked. Is it too painful to talk about?'

She shook her head.

'No. But I wish there were more I remembered.'

'You went down to the Dalesman, didn't you? About how long were you there?'

'Perhaps an hour. An hour and a quarter.'

'And when you got home, it was dark?'

'Yes, or very nearly. And there is practically no street lighting on the lane up to the cottage.'

'Were you nervous at night?'

'Good heavens, no. Perhaps when I first moved to Hutton—because I'd been used to living in a school, you know, with lots of people around me. But I'd given up feeling jittery long ago.'

'You didn't notice lights on in the cottage?'

'No. But I always left lights on in the hall and sitting-room. More cheerful to come home to.'

'So you let yourself in. What happened then?'

'Well, I hung my coat up. It had been drizzling earlier, and I'd taken it with me. Then . . . let me see . . . I went into the sitting-room. I was just about to go to the kitchen and make a nightcap when I thought I heard a noise from the other side of the cottage—where all the old stuff was, you know. But I didn't think about burglars—not at all. I thought it was cats. There's a big ginger tom marauds around there, and you know the sort of smells they leave if you let them get in. I thought I must have left a window open. So I went through the hall, opened the door—'

'Yes?'

'There was light coming into the room from the hall. I remember feeling some kind of obstruction, from behind the door. I just thought the carpet was up, or something . . . What did I do then? . . . Oh yes, I turned to put the light on, but before my hand got to the switch, this *shape* came at me from behind the door. I can't describe it any better than that. And before I knew anything it began to hit me—and then again, and again . . . It was terrible, terrible. Because I didn't lose consciousness at once, you see.'

'Yes, yes. Don't think about it. Try to think back a little, to before that. Obviously you didn't get much of a look at this shape . . .'

'No, hardly any at all. I was turned towards the light switch, you see.'

'But if you didn't actually *see* it, you may have got some *impression* of it. Of its size, for example.'

'Oh, dear—I don't know . . .'

'As big as me, for example?'

'Oh no. I don't think so. It would have come at me—hit me—so much from *above* if it had been.'

'Tell me, did you have a visit some days before the break-in, from religious canvassers—Seventh Day Adventists, or something?'

'Yes. Yes, I did. Norwegians, I think. I talked with them a little, just out of curiosity. But it was odd: they didn't seem to know much about the Bible.'

'No, I'm not surprised. Tell me, was the shape as big as those men, would you say?'

'No, I wouldn't think so. Really, now you come to press it, I don't think it was a very *big* person at all. Not awfully strong. Because if it was, he could have stunned me right away, don't you think? But he went on hitting—not *hard*, but *often*. Horrible! But I think he was frightened, and perhaps not used to violence. That seems funny, if it was some kind of professional burglar. But it was so—*random*, somehow. And frenzied. Like a child, you know.'

'You make me weep for him,' I said, thinking with distaste of the etiolated Timothy Scott-Windlesham, the reluctant thug, the amateur who takes minutes to stun his victim. There is something to be said for professionalism, even in thuggery.

'Miss Wing, there is one other thing I wanted to ask you about: your will—'

She sighed, as if very tired and sad.

'Oh yes. I've lain here wondering whether you'd look into that—whether you had the right . . .'

'We have no right. But I'm afraid your friend Mrs Hebden let something slip. And of course we were interested, because the will was obviously relevant.'

'But it *isn't* relevant. It has nothing to do with all this. And it would be so easy for silly people to get the wrong idea. I have nobody close, you see: a few cousins, but none I have any great contact with—except the Macklehoses, and the less contact I have *there* in the future, the better I'll like it. I don't see how anyone with a grain of religion in them could feel anything but contempt for him, and the rest of that branch of the family too.'

'I have my eyes on him lovingly,' I assured her. 'If I can get him for anything, I fully intend to.'

'Good. And all the better for those poor silly people who go to him, though I suppose they always drift along to some other crank or crook in the long run. Or get involved in politics. Well, as I said, I'm virtually alone, and I haven't got much, but what little I do have I didn't want to go back to the government, which heaven knows gets enough out of single people as it is. So I thought I'd leave it to someone I liked.'

'Of course. Perfectly sensible. You don't have to explain.'

'Oh, but I *do*. I wanted to leave it to someone I liked, who was also young. Because I've always worked with young people, and liked them. Now, I'm not a great brain, as you know, but I'm rarely wrong about children. A *nice* boy, and a lively mind too, if only his school would find it out and encourage it. *Not* well-educated, poor boy, but enquiring, which is the important thing. And it appealed to me to give it to someone who has been — what's the modern word? — disadvantaged . . . What awful things people do to the English language these days, don't they? . . . So I left a few mementoes to some of my old colleagues at Broadlands, and the rest to Jason.'

'Did you tell him this?'

'*Really*, Mr Trethowan, do you think I'm a complete fool? There's nothing so unsettling as knowing you're going to inherit something at some time, even if it's nothing very grand. Particularly for someone like Jason, who really has no expectations of that sort at all. No, it was entirely a secret between me and my lawyer. Until now,' she added, with some bitterness.

'The thing is, you see, that if the manuscript is what we think it might be, it changes you from a person of modest means into something like a very rich woman.'

'It certainly does not,' she said energetically. 'And even if it did, little Jason would certainly not realize the value of the manuscript. I doubt if any of the older people in Hutton-le-Dales would either, come to that. And, you know, if I had thought of selling the manuscript, I would have made a very different will, leaving the cottage and things to Jason, and distributing the rest to charities: I have some I contribute my mite to regularly.'

'Ah—I see. But you *didn't* think of selling?'

'No, indeed. What would I do with the sort of money that would fetch, if it's genuine? I'd feel almost indecent taking it, for something I'd come across almost accidentally. And then, you see, it would probably go out of the country.'

'Yes, indeed.'

'I wouldn't have wanted that. No, in so far as I'd decided anything, I intended to give it to the Haworth Parsonage Museum. Let them get some expert to edit it. I rather looked forward to all the publicity there would be, I admit. I've led a very retired life, Mr Trethowan, and the thought of all that excitement was like several gin and tonics. But beyond that, I didn't want to profit from the manuscript. I wouldn't have thought it right.'

'And you told this to—who?'

'I told everybody that. The people in the pub—'

'Mr Scott-Windlesham?'

'Yes, indeed. Self-righteous of me, perhaps, but I did tell everybody that was what I intended, if it should prove genuine.'

And thereby, I thought, very nearly knocked another nail in your coffin. But I just leaned over and shook her hand, and said goodbye. As I was going, she said, almost energetically:

'You're *not* going to go and badger Jason, are you?'

'I wasn't thinking of it.'

'I *know* you police ,' she said.

'I think you're going to get better,' I smiled.

CHAPTER 13

LEANING HEAVILY

The interview with Miss Wing was heartening, because she was a brave soul, and I liked her. But it was hardly heartening in any other way. It left the case very much where it had been. Her evidence didn't even rule out Jason Curle as her attacker: he did not know he was Miss Wing's heir, but he must have known about the manuscript. Probably everyone in the village who was not deaf or mentally defective knew about the manuscript. But I didn't dwell on Jason Curle, because I was dwelling, rather lovingly, on Timothy Scott-Windlesham as the frightened, frenzied attacker.

It was no doubt Miss Wing's firm declaration of intent, to give the manuscript to Haworth, that did it. He must have had his intuitive hopes when she showed him the pages, and no doubt he went away—just as Jan and I did—and did a bit of research afterwards, to establish likelihoods and possibilities. He too must have been convinced. He had come within a stone's throw of the literary discovery of the century, and if it went to Haworth he would be as far from participating in the glory, wealth and promotion that would flow from it as if he had never seen it. The lifeline to which he clung was Tetterfield, who was acquisitive, eccentric and unscrupulous enough to go in with him in any scheme. The two of them came to an agreement that Timothy procure the manuscript, which would then turn up some years hence, perhaps when Miss Wing was dead, in Tetterfield's chaotic collection. No one could easily dispute the possibility of that. And then Tetterfield could nominate little Timmy as editor — for by that time the Meredith expert could have moved sideways and backwards into Brontë territory, and could have qualified himself in Brontë studies by a note here on a textual crux, a little article there on images of vampirism in *Wuthering Heights* . . .

And yet, there seemed not much more to be done that was likely to confirm my guess. I could, of course, get a search warrant to go through Timothy's residence, wherever that might be, but I could hardly doubt that any blood-stained clothing would long since have been destroyed, and that no trace would exist of any connection with old Tetterfield. Timothy was unlovely and unlovable, but he was no fool. Nor were my suspicions so firmly grounded that I could easily justify applying for a search warrant.

I'd talked all this over on the phone with Jan, of course, but though she was scathing about my inaction and lack of progress, she had little to suggest herself beyond a checking of all the people who did contract typing in the North of England, in the hope that a typescript was being prepared before the thing was smuggled out of the country. I thanked her very much for the suggestion, and pointed out the numbers of people likely to be involved, and the practical difficulties any attempt along these lines was sure to encounter. She said I was a defeatist. I was beginning to think she was right.

A couple of days after the interview with Miss Wing I gave Jan my usual no-progress report over the phone and then went disconsolately to the Dalesman to have a lunch-time pint and an infra-red grilled steak pie of unutterable awfulness. When I got back to the cottage the phone was ringing, and went on ringing as I hurriedly let myself in. I caught it just before Jan gave up.

'Oh, *there* you are. You take your time. Are you mowing the lawn for want of anything better to do?'

'I was having my lunch. A pub lunch is a policeman's inalienable right, though if I have any more like the one I've just eaten, I think I'll be willing to give it up.'

'Yes, well, something came up at lunch-time here.'

'The food?'

'No, it was rather good. Mordred was cooking. Shut up, Perry, and don't distract me. This is serious. Do you remember your Uncle Lawrence once wrote his memoirs?'

'Oh God! Why do you have to bring up things like that? Yes, I do remember, dimly. Weren't they called *The Pen is Mightier*?'

'That's right.'

'And the *Guardian*, when they reviewed it, missed out the space between the second and third words, and he got in a fearful bate and threatened to sue. I expect they knew what they were doing. Anything less mighty than Uncle Lawrence's pen would be difficult to imagine.'

'Yes, anyway, the subject came up, I can't remember how . . . Oh yes, it was Aunt Kate complaining that Lawrence hadn't mentioned her once in that book.'

'I didn't think the old boy had so much discretion.'

'So Aunt Sybilla started going on about the trouble the book had caused, even though it only sold about ten copies. I think by then Uncle Lawrence was crippled with arthritis, and apparently his handwriting was in any case as indecipherable as the Rosetta Stone—'

'Just like his arrogance,' I put in.

'Yes, so it seems that the final manuscript was in quite an appalling mess, and Aunt Sybilla says that it had to be sent to "the cleverest little woman in Leeds, dear, can you imagine?" And even *she* made some mistakes that Lawrence was too lazy or too high-handed to pick up when he proof-read, so that when it came out it said he'd unceremoniously banged Queen Mary in an antique shop, instead of barged into— you know the sort of thing. Even more embarrassing if you correct it with an errata slip than if you don't.'

'Ah— hence the *Guardian* misprint, I suppose,' I said. 'But get back to the little woman.'

'I thought you'd be interested in her. Well, of course I asked who the little woman was, and Aunt Sybilla said, oh dear, what was it, such a *frightfully* clever little woman, though in the end she charged more than the book brought in, and so on and round and round, as she does. Finally Mordred went away— he's writing the family history, you know—'

'*A Family and its Fall*. Yes, I know.'

'— and he found all the letters from her, and her account. Her name is Selina Boothroyd, and she lived at number 45, Jubilee Parade, Leeds. The letters were all very formal, positively cold, in fact, and I didn't get much out of them, but apparently she's quite well known, and can decipher practically anything.'

'Hmmm,' I said. 'That might be worth following up. Leeds is a coincidence, after all. The clean-hands boys knew the Scands were being followed, that I might be led to this bird's house, so they told them to arrange the hand-over some place where there was too much bustle for it to be noticed. And at the tennis the lady was not taken too far out of her way. It's an idea, I must say. The only idea I've got at the moment. You know, Jan, I think I'll go after it.'

'I thought you would, Perry. You see, keeping contact with your family is worthwhile after all.'

'I'm not sure that a disgraceful lifetime is redeemed by a useful dotage,' I said. 'But all right, I'll go along with that: my family has its occasional uses, as well as its manifest and continual drawbacks.'

'Did you know your sister had taken up writing?'

'Oh no!'

'Yes. She's writing for Bills and Coo, the romantic publishers. Does it while she's watching over baby in the garden. She's on one now called *Forbidden Fruits*.'

'Oh God! The next thing we know she'll be guzzling honey. See what I mean about a family and its fall?'

And I banged down the receiver, once again happily ill-humoured about my family and its doings.

But I didn't stay crabby for long. The more I thought about it, the more I liked Jan's gobbet of information. It was a logical step for Parfitt and Waddington to get a typescript made before trying to spirit the manuscript out of the country. And, if I'd thought about it properly, I would have realized that just any old typist simply wouldn't do: they would inevitably make a hash out of the tiny script unless they had extensive experience of problem manuscripts. That, obviously, was what the Boothroyd woman could offer, and it sounded as if she could afford to price herself high. And if she turned out not to be the one, she could surely put me on to others in her line of country, people who offered the same sort of service. I took down the telephone directory and looked her up: Boothroyd, S., 45 Jubilee Parade, Leeds. I was just putting my finger in the dial when some instinct told me this was too important a matter to leave to the telephone. Probably Selina Boothroyd was a timid old lady. I have been known to charm timid old ladies. I have also been known to scare the wits out of them. I decided to pay her a visit.

It was still early in the afternoon, and I decided to make a detour on the way. I dropped in at the Police Headquarters at Milltown and had a word with Capper, the inspector I'd spoken to when I first arrived. He was decidedly less harassed since the departure of the Prime Minister, but I had the impression that he was still very happy to leave everything to me, in a case whose literary ramifications gave him that bullish, aggressive feeling that people who don't read do get when confronted with bookish matters. But he had some stuff for me about Rolf Tingvold and Knut Ratikainen — stuff hot from the FBI. They had indeed been seamen, thrown off a super-tanker five years before as troublemakers. The captain had described Ratikainen as a psychopath, and his subsequent career had gone some way to proving his point. He and Tingvold had drifted into the New York crime world, and had quickly proved themselves as reliable heavies, strong on intimidation and exemplary violence. Ratikainen, in particular, had executed with relish some particularly beastly jobs. He had served a one-year gaol sentence in New York, where he had quickly established a nasty sort of dominance over a community not noted for peaceable diffidence. Since then they had been on hire, and had built up their reputations as the criminal equivalents of a Scandinavian car: tough, quiet and reliable. And, in their case, very brutal.

'But as far as the New York police are concerned, Parfitt is out of it,' Capper said, with that depressing police determination not to tangle with men of power if he could avoid it. 'No connection of any kind with these two thugs, or with things of this sort in general.'

'No doubt,' I sighed. 'And no doubt that's how he'll keep it. Is he still in the area?'

'No. He's gone to Edinburgh.'

'He won't get any bargains there. He's distancing himself, I suppose. Very fly, is Mr Parfitt. Probably he regards this job as virtually in the bag. What about the two thugs — I suppose they've dissolved themselves into thin air?'

'Well — I'm afraid they have. The Leeds police couldn't afford the men to keep a twenty-four-hour watch on them. They clocked out of their guest-house and left, and by the time the proprietor had contacted the police, there was no trail to follow. For all they know they may be anywhere in the country—may have left it, in fact. The only thing is, one of the Leeds constables—the bloke who helped you take them at the tennis—thinks he's seen them in Briggate.'

'Hopeful.'

'That was two days ago. Any point in putting out an alert?'

'None. I've no more on them now than I had when I grilled them. If I do get anything, I'll let you know. At the moment I'm going to visit a lady typist.'

'A typist? Oh—you think they may be getting the thing written out proper, like?'

'It's a chance. I'd like to bet the woman—if this is the one—will have been sworn to total secrecy. I may have to play it by ear—see what kind of a soul she is. People of that sort don't often like getting involved with the criminal world. Appeals to conscience might work—or alternatively, coming the heavy might be necessary.'

'Ah well,' said Capper. 'They don't work by the rule book in Leeds.'

'That's rather what I hoped,' I said, and took my leave.

Of course, I wasn't actually contemplating beating up Selina Boothroyd. Beating up old ladies is something I've rarely been called on to do in the course of my career, and when I have, I've derived little enjoyment from it. However, one can come the heavy cop with startling effect at times, particularly with the weak and timid. On the other hand, I had no notion whether Selina Boothroyd would turn out to be weak or timid, or even what age she might be. I had the impression she had not let my Uncle Lawrence get the better of her, so perhaps she would not be a pushover after all.

Jubilee Parade was in the oddly named Hyde Park area. It didn't seem to have much to do with our own dear open space. It was a turning off Cardigan Road: I gathered much of the land around here had been owned by the Earl of Cardigan — he who had valiantly led his men into the Valley of Death, and then (most unfairly) ridden out of it practically alone. I drove around Jubilee Parade several times, and then parked my car round a corner out of sight.

No. 45 was a house not unlike old Tetterfield's in Bradford: a three-storey Victorian job, of rather discoloured brick, and surrounded by the sort of dark evergreens that add privacy rather than beauty to a garden, and seem to be striving to get the upper hand over the gardener. These had definitely got the upper hand. The windows of the house were small and grudging, but even if they had been larger the shrubs would have prevented much light from getting in. Most of the houses on Jubilee Parade were like this — well separated from their neighbours, with greenery dating from the time they had all been family houses. But most of them now seemed to be divided up, many of them inhabited by students and suchlike, and some seemed to house more than one Asian family. No. 45 was rather more run-down than the rest, and the total effect was desolate bordering on the eeries. I shook off the feeling. Victorian houses in the suburbs of Leeds might have draughts and musty smells, but I shouldn't turn them into something out of late Hitchcock.

I pushed open the gate, which stuck, and then swung loosely on its hinges. The front door was a brown-painted affair, peeling, with a lead-lighted window in a design of flowers unknown to botany. From somewhere inside I could hear the sound of high-speed typing, punctuated by longish pauses. So far, so hopeful. But then, she could equally be typing a sociological thesis. The knocker was stiff and unusable, but finally I found a bell tucked away in the brown paint, and put my finger on it.

There was silence in the house, and then I heard the sound of slippered feet advancing along the hallway. The door opened a fraction.

'Yes?'

'Oh, are you Miss Boothroyd?'

'Yes.'

'I wonder if I may come in and speak to you?'

'If you're selling anything, I'm not interested.'

'I'm not selling anything. It's about a manuscript.'

She opened the door a fraction more.

'Oh, if it's about a job—'

'It's not exactly a job I have for you. It's a manuscript that may have been given to you to type. A very old one.'

There was a pause.

'Well, I wouldn't know anything about that.'

'Miss Boothroyd, I am a policeman—'

There came over her face an expression of dismay, in which was mingled fear—obvious, unconcealable fear. She let the door swing open a little more, and I put my foot in the opening. Now I could get a look at her for the first time. She was a faded scrap of gentility in a muddy mauve woollen dress, with lacklustre hair that was fading from fair to grey, without ever having been attractive in either shade. It was a tired, troubled face, giving the impression of one for whom worry was a way of life. I thought I'd seen her before, but in her generation—she was, I guessed, in her late fifties—one still found plenty of these disappointed, repressed, slightly hysterical spinsters (and bachelors) whom life seemed not just to have passed by, but given a contemptuous kick to in passing. Probably in a generation or two the type will virtually have died out—unless, as I sometimes suspect, the permissive society does not exist outside a two mile radius of central London. I imagined Miss Boothroyd staying on in the house where she had been born, as the rest of the family died out or moved away, finding it much too big for her, but resisting the thought of moving, and clinging on to all the things that reminded her of childhood, when she had life and activity and people around her. I had no desire to cling to my childhood, but I understood the instinct to cling. Miss Boothroyd's charges seemed to be high. How far would she be willing to go, if the price was right?

'Perhaps we could go inside, Miss Boothroyd?'

'Do you have a search warrant?'

'No—'

'Then I can't let you in. I'm alone in the house. How do I know you're a policeman?'

I showed her my identification.

'Nevertheless . . .' she said. 'We can talk quite well here.'

I sighed. 'Very well. As I said, what I'm investigating is a manuscript that has disappeared.'

'I told you, I wouldn't know anything about that.'

'It was stolen.'

She blinked, but resumed her obstinate expression: 'Well, I'm very sorry, but I don't know why you should come to me.'

'I haven't described the manuscript to you yet. Perhaps you should not deny knowledge of it till you know what it looks like. It's a very old one. Large sheets of paper, folded several times. They are covered with very tiny writing, almost unreadable. It is a novel, or part of one. One of the characters is called Thomas Blackmore. There's a place called Lingdale Manor in it.'

'I don't know anything about it,' she repeated.

'It would be a very difficult manuscript to transcribe, which is why I thought they might have come to you.'

'Well, they didn't,' she said, her voice rising, and taking on an edge, close to tears. 'There are plenty of others who do this sort of thing. Why did you come to me?'

'I thought of you because you once transcribed a manuscript of my uncle Lawrence — Lawrence Trethowan.' I offered this as a delicate branch of friendship.

'That was a disgusting book,' she burst out, flinging the branch back in my face. 'It was positively unclean. He ought to have been ashamed, sending a thing like that to a lady.'

'My uncle was like that,' I said, not wishing to get into an argy with the moral majority. 'Now, as I told you, this manuscript was stolen —'

'I don't know why you go on. I've told you I know nothing about it. I'm a busy woman with a living to earn, so will you please go away —'

'It was stolen in circumstances of great brutality.' This time she flinched, good and openly. 'I would like you to know the sort of person you may be dealing with. The lady who owned the manuscript, a lady some years older than yourself, was physically attacked, and so ferociously that she is only beginning to come round now, a fortnight later. Her wounds were so serious that her life was despaired of.'

Now there was no mistaking it. Her expression had become one of naked fear, and her hand was shaking on the doorknob.

'Another person who had the manuscript in his possession was beaten up, very sadistically, over a long period of time, to make him give it up.'

'Please stop it! I don't want to hear about these horrors!'

'But I think you should, Miss Boothroyd. Do you think it sensible to get mixed up in something of this kind? To get involved with the sort of people who would do things like that? Because you may feel safe with the people who employ you, but there is more than one lot involved. Are you safe from the rest of them? Can your thugs protect you from the other thugs?'

'You're treating me like a criminal!'

'Now that you've been told what you're involved in, you would be a criminal if you continued with what you're doing. I'm telling you for your own protection. And if you're sensible you surely will admit that no amount of money could compensate for the mental pressure you've been putting yourself under.'

'Stop it! Stop it!' she almost shrieked. 'I've told you, I don't know anything about any manuscript—'

'Then why are you getting so worked up?' I asked. I leaned forward ingratiatingly. 'Miss Boothroyd, there's no possible blame attaching to you in this matter—so far. Now, why don't you let me in, and we can discuss—'

But unfortunately in leaning forward persuasively I had taken my foot out of the door, and she banged it shut, fetching me a hefty clump on the nose. I'd make a rotten salesman. I shouted through the door: 'You do realize you're putting your own life in danger, don't you, you silly woman?'

There were hysterical sobs from inside, and then:

'Go away! Leave me alone! I won't put up with this persecution.'

I waited, hoping my words would sink in. There was silence from inside, then the sound of someone going upstairs. Going to lie down on the bed and have a good cry, I thought. So ended my attempt to lean heavily on the weak and feeble. I was annoyed with myself, but more aggravated by the stupidity of the woman: the fact is, there *is* no one stupider than someone who has seen an unexpected windfall landing in their lap, and then has to contemplate it eluding their grasp after all.

I went down to the gate, and then out into the road. Somehow I was going to have to get into that house. The sheer suspiciousness of Selina Boothroyd's behaviour had probably justified me in applying for a search warrant. But that took time. Had I got it? Not if Miss Boothroyd got on the phone to her employers. I felt the manuscript had eluded me often enough already in this case.

I walked down Jubilee Parade, and a dreary, unfestive parade it seemed to me now. At the end, at the corner of Cardigan Road, there was a phone-box, and I decided to ring up Jan and tell her the success of her inspired guess. I had only just got through and was launching into the story when I saw stirrings down the road at No. 45. Over the shrubs I could just see the front door open, and someone come out.

'Hang on, Jan,' I said, 'I think something's happening.'

I leant low over the phone, but Miss Boothroyd was coming along on the other side of the road, and by the distraught style of her walk it seemed unlikely that she would see anybody. She was wearing a large felt hat with a feather in it, and clutching a brown hold-all.

It was then that I realized why I'd had the idea that I'd seen her before. She was the woman who had sat in front of me at the Tabernacle of the Risen Moses.

CHAPTER 14

BREAKING AND ENTERING

As she went past I started muttering nonsense into the phone to Jan, the mouthpiece cradled in my shoulder, my arm covering my face. Oh yes—it was her all right: the hat was unmistakable. It was the woman who had sat in front of me at the Macklehose religious rites, and it was the member of the congregation I'd seen at the tennis. And as I thought back I remembered more. What was it she had cried out? Something about greed. She'd mentioned lust for gold. She'd looked into her heart and found lust for gold. Oh yes, Sister Boothroyd—I believe you!

Sister Boothroyd . . . Now I remembered Amos Macklehose's good-nights on the porch of his spiritual hovel. 'See you on Tuesday, Sister Boothroyd,' he had said. 'It will do you good.' That was a facer. What was the betting the silly woman had been to him and *confessed*? Told him what she was doing? This raised all sorts of unpleasant possibilities. She could even be taking the thing to him now . . .

' 'Bye, Jan — ring as soon as I can,' I gabbled, and I slammed down the phone and emerged from the box as Miss Boothroyd went out of sight round the corner.

I dashed to the corner and peered round a privet hedge, down the traffic-ridden expanses of Cardigan Road. She was waiting at a bus stop. She was clutching her hold-all so desperately that she seemed to be trying to pull it apart, her hands working vigorously and hysterically the whole time. She kept looking down the road in my direction, and I had to keep darting back behind cover. Within a couple of minutes she was rewarded. A bus came along, going to the centre. She darted on as if she were being pursued by a troop of mounties. As the bus drove off I dashed down Jubilee Parade and found the turning where I had parked my car. In half a minute I was after the bus.

I was on tenterhooks that she would get out before it had finished its run, and dash into somewhere that would turn out to be the Reverend Macklehose's manse. But she didn't. In little over ten minutes the bus drew up at City Station and she got out, still looking more than a little dazed and distressed. I left the car in the forecourt, any old how, and leapt after her.

By the time I caught up with her she had her ticket, and was heading in the direction of Platform Three. There was nothing to be done but catch her up and stop her.

'Miss Boothroyd!'

'*Oh!*' She jumped, looked round, then broke into a flood of tears. 'You're persecuting me! I shall complain to my MP. What *right* have you to follow me in this way? I've done nothing wrong. You said so yourself. You're treating me like a *criminal!*'

People began looking at her, and edging away from us.

'Miss Boothroyd, I don't think you're a criminal, but I do think someone has involved you in criminal business. Do you mind telling me where you're going?'

'I'm going to Scarborough. To stay with my sister. I can't — I can't stand it anymore. The strain, the worry. The *persecution* — by the police, who are supposed to protect us. I've got to get away.'

'That's probably the wisest thing you've done in a long time. But just one more thing: can I search your bag?'

'*Oh!* This is too much. To be searched like a common thief in a public place. Oh — oh, take it.'

She threw the bag at me, and broke into another uncontrollable fit of sobbing. To add to her public humiliation, the bits and pieces of personal belongings and underwear scattered all over the platform. I put my hand in the bag and felt around, but the manuscript was not there. Together we got down on our knees on the grimy platform and tried to put Miss Boothroyd together again into a middle-class lady of unimpeachable rectitude. But in the end we had to scramble everything together and bundle her past the ticket-collector and on to the train. She ran frantically down the platform, never once looking back. I suppose I couldn't have expected a vote of thanks.

At any rate that was her out of the way, and — it was to be hoped — out of danger. The next thing was to get back to the house. Darkness was some way off, but it would come. Meanwhile I wanted to see that no one got into that house. I wanted to keep that house safe for me.

Back in Jubilee Parade things were quiet and early

eveningy — a mixture of dusk and dust, with lawns being mown and television sets winking through the windows. A few students came out, on studently errands to discos and pubs, no doubt, most of them catching the bus from Miss Boothroyd's stop in Cardigan Road. Other than that, few were about. I left my car in the little side-street off the Parade, and ensconced myself in the telephone kiosk. As I expected, Jan was desperately waiting for my call, and thoroughly agog.

'Perry, what on earth is happening? Suddenly you start muttering like a madman and then you go off the line. Are you trying to drive me crazy or something?'

I told her what had been going on, and where I now was.

'Poor old thing,' said Jan. 'It sounds as if you've practically driven her over the brink.'

'OK — poor old thing. But why should middle-class people expect the sort of kid-glove treatment which they'd hate us to give your average street thug? She did everything except remind me that she paid her taxes. Most people seem to regard that as exempting them from suspicion. At best this old duck was silly. At worst — well, she's an intelligent woman, or she couldn't do the job she does do. Don't tell me she didn't know what she was doing when she agreed to do the job for the Scands. Did she think it was all in a day's work when she agreed to receive the manuscript in the way she did? And when she found that it was old, and probably valuable — didn't she have a faint whiff of suspicion? I bet they offered her a mint of money for doing it.'

'So they ought to have. But it's obvious she was feeling guilty even before you came.'

'Nervous, anyway. All right — probably guilty too. The dregs of the good old British Nonconformist conscience. When that sort of conscience is really reduced to the dregs it goes batty, and starts frequenting places like the

Tabernacle of the Risen Moses. That's the thing I'm most afraid of: that Miss Boothroyd has opened her heart to the dreadful Amos. I refuse to call it confession. Blabbing might be the word.'

'You don't think he's given up?'

'I do not. I think he'd come after it. That is, if he isn't in it with James L. Parfitt himself. That's something I just can't make up my mind about.'

'But, Perry, are you going to stick around there like a stuffed owl all night? What's the point?'

'I'm not. I'm just waiting till dark.'

'Then what?'

'Oh, then I'm going in.'

'You're not, Perry! Without a warrant?'

'Warrants take time. I've been told,' I said carefully, 'that they don't worry too much about the rule book, in Leeds.'

'But, Perry, it could be dangerous. You might —'

But I put down the phone on that. Of course I intended to take all precautions. But I felt that at last I had the case under control, and from now on I was going to make the running. Now all I had to do was wait until dark.

But nothing is slower in coming than night on a summer evening. I dallied in the telephone booth for a bit, but before long another user appeared. I strolled up and down Jubilee Parade, loitered on the corners, inspected the houses and gardens as if I were interested in buying property. Gradually the lawn-mowers ceased to hum, and were cleaned and put away in garages and sheds. More television sets started winking in the windows as more people settled down in front of the evening news, to get their statistics on unemployment and inflation, the chirpings of comfort and doom from politicians. The odd car drove up, bringing people from pubs and cinemas. A few upstairs lights went on as children were put to bed.

Finally cloud began to come up, to hasten the twilight process. The light became tenuous, the air heavy. I walked round to my parked car, and fetched a torch. In those final minutes before night fell I strolled once more along Jubilee Parade, hell of a casual, and then pushed open the sticky gate of No. 45 and let myself into the gloomy garden.

The late-Victorian middle-classes certainly had a way with a garden. It was all very well for Wordsworth to babble about the spiritual benefits of one impulse from a vernal wood. He never tried it with a suburban shrubbery. As I crept along the front of the house all sorts of heavy, green-black leaves, shiny and unpleasant, brushed my face. The darkness suddenly seemed impenetrable. I had to duck to avoid sudden, unexpected overhanging branches. Round the side of the house the overgrowth thinned a little, and I could just see, through a gap, the living-room of the house next door. The family were crouched in front of one of those American police series where the credit titles are so long and arty that it's time for the commercial break before they're over. I didn't think I needed to fear interference from that quarter.

I parted fronds, and plodded cautiously ahead to the back garden. A weedy tentacle caught my foot, and I went sprawling into a mass of nettles. I repressed the blasphemy that rose to my lips (who said one was close to God in a garden?) and ploughed on. At the back of the house there was an overgrown lawn, but by now it was as totally dark as the front. Totally dark and still. So it was too on the other side of the house. I lingered on the lawn. The back garden seemed to abut on a similar garden on another street. I needn't, presumably, expect any incursions from that direction. The house was completely dark. The problem now was how to get in.

The obvious way was to start trying the windows. Miss

Boothroyd had left in a hurry and a state of hysteria, and was all too likely to have left one unfastened. On the other hand, the vision of myself doing a sneak-in similar to that of Amos Macklehose at Miss Wing's cottage was not an enticing one. If I knew Miss Boothroyd, she was a typical middle-class householder, and as a policeman I know that your typical middle-class householder usually has a spare key hidden somewhere. Somewhere, be it said, where any burglar with half a brain can find it. And what any burglar can do, any burglarious policeman can do too. So much more dignified, I thought, to go in through the front door. I edged my way back through the undergrowth, towards the front of the house.

There I was much more exposed than at the back. There was a street-light no more than a few yards up the road. I lingered under an evergreen of a particularly aggressive kind. The light enabled me to get a good look at the front porch. The usual resort of the feeble-minded was the front-door mat. Miss Boothroyd was not so silly. Over the door, on the top ledge, was a possibility. But she was not that tall, and I guessed she would only just be able to reach there. There were two geranium pots on either side of the porch. Those seemed very good bets. What say she would put it under the one to her right hand as she came out of the front door?

I strolled up to the porch, raised the pot with an air of casual authority, felt under it, extracted the key, and let myself in by the front door as if I were a helpful friend, come to water the pot plants. Easy as winking.

But inside was pitch dark. I was fairly sure I had not been seen coming in, so there was no point in advertising my presence. Miss Boothroyd could well have phoned a neighbour and asked her to keep an eye on the place. I had not been able to get a look at the hall through the crack in the door Miss Boothroyd had vouchsafed me on our interview. I had to switch on my torch. Cautiously I played it round the walls. It was very much the sort of place one would expect: a chiming clock, ticking authoritatively and showing the wrong time; lots of dark varnish; and the sort of wall-paper that seems to be aspiring to the condition of dark varnish.

I flashed the torch along, keeping the beam close to the floor. To the right, the front room. The best room, no doubt. Miss Boothroyd certainly had not been typing there — the noise had come from further off. I advanced a few steps. To the left was the staircase. Shabby carpeting, getting stringy and dangerous in places. I went further forwards. Two other doorways: to the left, the kitchen, to the right — what? The other living-room, probably — doubling, perhaps, as a study, to save on heating? This seemed to be the best bet. I pushed open the door. Through the window, sailing above the acacias and laurels, the moon gazed pale and solemn through the window. I extinguished the torch and went over to pull the curtains. They were heavy and old, velvet with worn pile. I tugged the cord at their side and they slid closed. Now I felt well shut in, insulated. I put the torch on again and flashed it with more confidence.

It was a big room, damp and chill. Dark too, at the best of times, I guessed. The armchairs were deep, heavy and springy: you could see the round marks of the springs through the covers. The desk was not by the window but near the door, facing the wall. No distraction, no deviation from the work in hand — unless one could call a mildewed print of Landseer's *Hawking in the Olden Time* a distraction. In the centre of the desk an upright, heavy, manual typewriter. And on either side . . . I went over to it, my heart beating.

On the right side, face downwards, was the transcript. Two hundred and fifty pages of it. Industrious Miss Boothroyd! Money-hungry Miss Boothroyd! On either end of the desk, two piles — one large, one small. Square, brown, aged sheets of paper, folded and roughly torn at the edges. As I gazed at them, Miss Boothroyd's dark room, Jubilee Parade, Leeds itself, faded to nothingness, and I remembered seeing other tiny manuscript books on that visit to Haworth Parsonage; and as my mind went back to that July visit two years ago I remembered the moors outside, and that endless purple blanket of heather, its blinding, incongruously regal splendour.

My heart seemed to contract, my whole body stand still, as if I had caught a first glimpse of something or somebody overwhelmingly beautiful. I took the large pile in my hands. A feeling flowed through me that was almost sexual. I turned over the sheets of the typescript. She had done the first three-quarters or so of the novel, with only twenty-odd sheets left in the small pile of manuscript. There was no title, but the words Chapter I were written at the top of the page. I brought my torch closer and peered at the opening words:

That summer, the summer of my twenty-second year, was the last summer of my content. July and August had been hot, with blazing sun and a heavy air . . .

Suddenly my torch was no longer the only light in the room. Two shafts of light from the door illuminated an automatic and a long, gleaming knife. And above the knife was the impassive, Mongolian face of the Norwegian Finn, his eyes sparkling in the torchlight.

'Ah, Mr Police. I said I would know you again.'

CHAPTER 15

GRIEVOUS BODILY HARM

'Put it down, Mr Police,' said Knut Ratikainen. 'Put it down on the desk where you got it from.'

He had a soft, silky voice, almost a purr. You didn't have to dislike cats to dislike his voice.

'And then put your hands on head,' said Rolf Tingvold. 'You done enough trouble for today.'

I meditated some kind of action with my feet. There seemed a choice between kicking at the knife and getting a bullet in my ribs, and kicking at the gun and getting a knife in my ribs. Both feet at once was the sort of Bruce Lee stuff I couldn't manage. I put my hands on my head and decided to delay things with a little light conversation, in the traditional manner.

'Trouble?' I said. 'What kind of trouble was that? Upset Miss Boothroyd before she had finished the job, I suppose? Very worrying for you. Mr Parfitt will not be pleased.'

'All those names, just like before. We never heard of this guy. You talk nonsenses. Is not important, anyway. Plenty of typists in the world.'

'Lucky she'd got so far,' I said. 'Fast worker she must be.'

'With us to hurry her up,' said Ratikainen, with a nasty snigger.

'Oh, you've been here all the time, have you? That must have been cosy for her. She looked the type who'd really appreciate having chaps like you in her house.'

'Two days,' said Tingvold. 'Since we knew we'd shaken off your people. We thought we might as well keep a watch over our property. Keep the work going well.'

'That rather explains her nervous condition, then. Anyway, why worry about that? Mr Parfitt will be proud of you. Millionaires like employees who keep their noses to the grindstone.'

'What's this about noses? You talk riddles, as usual. We do this for ourselves. For our love of literature, eh, Knut? Still, it's nice to have a little chat. Cosy, like you say. We been waiting for this.'

'I been waiting for it,' said Ratikainen.

'Knut's been waiting. Knut, he's very good with little chats. But in this case we don't expect much from you. You haven't got anything we want.'

'Unlike Tetterfield,' I said.

'Unlike poor old Tetterfield. What a brave man! Even the best Knut could do was not enough. He never told us anything. We had to find the thing ourselves.'

'With Tetterfield you struck lucky,' I said. 'He wouldn't talk to us.'

'He thought he still got it,' said Tingvold, with a sneer. 'He laid in that hospital and he thought he still got it. He thought it was worth going through all that.'

'Tetterfield was different,' said Ratikainen, flicking his tongue round his lips. 'I had to be sure Tetterfield didn't die.'

I didn't like the unspoken corollary.

'Well, well,' said Tingvold. 'We don't think we leave till maybe two, three in the night. Very dark. Everybody sleep. That give us four, five hours, right? We can have fun, eh?'

'Anyone for Scrabble?' I said, feeling a bit like Albert Campion.

'Where shall we take him, Rolf?' said Ratikainen. 'What say we take him upstairs? We can put the light on in the landing. Nobody see. Then Mr Police can see what happen to him. Watch it all in slow motion, like the football on the television. Perhaps we put him in the bath, eh, Rolf? I like the bath game.'

'Whatever you say, Knut,' said his obedient side-kick. 'I always enjoy your shows. What say we tie him up first? Truss him up like a chicken, eh?'

'Just the hands, Rolf. Maybe a gag, so he don't make too much noise. Not that it matters much. If he does, the neighbours think it's the television. Nice gangster show. I tie him up, Rolf.'

He took his knife firmly in his hand and came towards me. If it had been him left covering me I might have tried something. But the revolver glimmered in the torchlight, and there is something very final about a revolver. Ratikainen took the collar of my jacket in his left hand and slit it down the back with his knife. Then he pulled it over my head. He went out into the kitchen to fetch some rope. He jerked my hands down, and tied them behind my back. It was coarse, hairy rope. It would be. It chafed like hell. The really nasty thing was when he came round in front of me again and looked into my face. The broad, impassive face was changed: he was practically slobbering with anticipation. Then he went into the kitchen again, and fetched a tea-towel. He tied it tightly round and in my mouth. It smelt of stale food, and seemed to be going right down my throat. I retched with nausea. Ratikainen kicked me, as if I ought to be showing gratitude.

Then Tingvold came round behind me, and prodded me with the gun.

'Get going,' he said.

I started out into the hall in an eerie silence. Their torches lit the way, but I stumbled on the frayed carpet of the stairs. Ratikainen kicked me again. Tingvold picked out every stair with the beam of his torch, and on and up we marched. It felt a bit like getting out of the tumbril and walking up the steps to the waiting invention of the good Dr Guillotine. Though one thing you could say for the guillotine: it was fast.

Up on the landing, Tingvold went around closing all the doors to the bedrooms. Then he switched on the landing light. A dim bulb of low wattage hardly made the scene more comfortable. Knut Ratikainen's face acquired menacing shadows. It had resumed its impassive expression, but the eyes seemed to sparkle more.

'We put him in the bathroom, eh, Rolf? Put him on the seat, then run a bath. Maybe the British police need a bit of cleaning up. I think that's what we do.'

So they shoved me forward into the bathroom, and sat me down on the lavatory. The dim light from the landing just penetrated here, so they pulled down a blind. Then they tied my feet. Knut Ratikainen stood over me with his knife, while Rolf Tingvold ran the bath. The cold tap. In the quarter light the dark water looked as uninviting as the Dead Sea. He turned off the tap, and the two of them stood there waiting, in that eerie silence. They enjoyed the silence. It was one of their weapons.

'What we do,' said Ratikainen, putting his face close to mine, 'is, we shove you in, then we shove you under, and we hold you there till your lungs are bursting. Then we let you up, and you get a few breaths of air — right? — and then we shove you down again and the game begins again. That's a real nice game. Real fun game. That's just to freshen you up for what comes after. You like that. What comes after. P'raps I give you a little taste of that in advance, eh?'

For some reason there flashed through my mind a picture of my father. Perhaps I was thinking how much he would have enjoyed this. But as it did so, Ratikainen leant over, ever so slowly, and took hold of my shirt. He ripped it down slowly to the waist.

'Shine the torch, Rolf, so he can see.'

And he put the knife down against my abdomen. Then, forcing himself against my legs to prevent my kicking, he delicately pushed it in an inch or so, then slowly, lovingly, twisted the knife round. I tried to scream with the pain, but the gag choked me. Ratikainen kept his face close to mine, watching me, the ends of his mouth turned upwards in a parody of a smile. Saliva gathered at the corners of his mouth. Then he slowly took the knife out, and wiped it on the rags of my shirt.

'You see? Just a little taste. Show you what we can do. I been looking forward to this, you can't imagine, Mr Police. Ever since the tennis I been looking forward to this. Shall we try another game now? Another little bit of fun? Or shall we have one more little bit of knife fun first?'

And he pushed himself against me again, and started bringing the knife slowly forward, a few inches above the first wound. He was just about to shove it in, when there was a noise from downstairs.

The two of them jerked upright, and stood frozen to the spot like two bits of monumental masonry from Vigeland Park. If I'd been in the mood to laugh, it would have been rather funny. Like one of those moments in a Rossini opera when, at the height of the brouhaha, there's a knocking at the door or something, and everyone goes completely quiet, and starts whispering '*Che sara?*' or whatever in unison. But, as I say, I wasn't in chuckling mood at the time.

The noise came again.

'Window!' said Rolf Tingvold.

'Downstairs,' said Ratikainen. 'The manuscript.'

They moved to the bathroom door and out on to the landing with a speed and silence that was creditable in men their size. I heard them move to the head of the staircase. Shafts of light were still coming in from the landing, but I heard a tiny creak as they began to move down the stairs. Fine—I still had some light. I looked around me, and fiddled my fingers to see that there was still feeling in them. There was a little pair of nail scissors on the edge of the bath. Useless. Bathrooms are the silliest places to get oneself tied up in. Nothing in the way of sharp knives at all. Then I saw, on the shelf above the washbasin, Miss Boothroyd's lady's razor. Not the equal of a cut-throat, but at least she hadn't gone electric. If only I could get it, and, having got it, not drop it. I stood up, manœuvred myself over to the washbasin, stood tiptoe against it and grasped the handle of the razor in my tied hands. The wound in my stomach sent shafts of pain darting through my body. I clutched firmly to the razor handle, and the pain began to abate. I sat down on the edge of the bath. Warm blood was oozing again over my shirt and the top of my trousers, but I took no notice. Worse things than flesh wounds were going to happen to me if I didn't get free. I began to work the blade of the fragile little razor over one strand of the rope. One strand, thank God, would be enough.

Suddenly I was startled out of my wits by a crash, and shouting, from downstairs. I nearly dropped the razor, but clutched on to it at the last moment and went on shaving away at the rope for dear life. Please God the fighting didn't bring them upstairs. Every stroke I made with it hurt my wrists, from the harshness of the rope still around them. From downstairs there was sudden silence. I was beginning to find silence menacing. The rope began to get looser. Suddenly, just as it seemed to be getting intolerably urgent, the one strand came apart. I had got through. I pulled my hands apart and the rope fell off. I brought my hands round to my front and began to rub life into my wrists. I bent down—God, the pain!—and pulled furiously at the rope around my ankles. When it came loose, I threw the rope aside, grabbed a hand towel and shoved it around my bleeding stomach, wrenched the gag from my mouth and slipped out on to the landing.

Silence, still, from downstairs. If only Miss Boothroyd

had had a phone extension upstairs I could have got help. I peered into each of the bedrooms, turned on the lights. No. I didn't expect it. Selina Boothroyd was emphatically not the type who went in for phone extensions. At the top of the stairs I listened. All was not so silent as I had thought. Talk was going on downstairs. Talk of a kind. It came in bursts, some of them loud. Then there were long pauses—tense, Pinterish silences. Some kind of negotiation, it seemed, was going on. At any rate the Scands hadn't squashed the intruder into the floorboards. Another burst of talk came. Could I get down the stairs during those bursts and out of the front door to the phone-box without being heard? I wasn't too sure. On the other hand, the options weren't enticing. Do a Tarzan through the evergreens from the bedroom window and risk them coming straight out and taking me? Stay upstairs and wait for little endearing to do another corkscrew job on my abdomen? Anything was better than that. If only Miss Boothroyd had a weapon of some kind. But it wasn't worth investigating. I didn't believe the maiden ladies of Leeds had yet started sleeping with a gun beside their beds.

I started off down the stairs.

By some blessed dispensation they did not creak. I kept to the sides, but by now the talk in the back room was becoming less sporadic. There were several voices, several different brands of hum. With infinite precaution I gained the bottom, and stood irresolute in the hall. Should I make for the front door and get help? Help could be an awfully long time coming. The voices from the back room were now audible, and they shook my resolution to get out—they enticed me, like sirens' songs. Through the half-open door at the other end of the passage I could see splashes of torchlight, and some dark, lowering shapes. Clearly the two sides were split up, one group by the window, the other by the door.

A wavering torch beam gave me a glimpse of the desk, with the manuscript in two piles at either end of it. I didn't want to leave it. My decision was made for me by the voice of Amos Macklehose, rising above the subdued hum. It was now less stage-parsonical than when he had talked to me, and it veered between broad North Country and the vernacular of California. It was still not an attractive voice, but it doubtless expressed the real Amos. I listened like a three years' child.

'You seem to forget who started all this. Perhaps you haven't been told. Well, it was me gave your boss the info. He'd never have heard about this if it 'adn't been for me.'

'We don't know nothing about that,' said Rolf Tingvold. 'You talk it over with him, right?'

'Oh yes — talk it over with him. Where would that get me? Even if I could find him to talk to, which he'd make good and sure I couldn't, I know what I'd get: "I've never soiled my hands with anything dubious —" and all that baloney. I had all that in his reply to my letter. "Mr Parfitt thanks you for the information, and would be interested in acquiring the item you mention from its legal owner. But he asked me to emphasize that in no eventuality could he engage in a transaction of uncertain legality." Him and his eventualities! Toffee-nosed git! I knew some classy stinkers in California, but California class wears hobnail boots compared to your East Coast aristocracy!'

It seemed to occur to Rolf Tingvold that Macklehose was in no position to be sure who his employers were. He said:

'Well, you take that up with this Parfitt, whoever he is. And we get on with our job, right?'

'Don't give me that —' began Amos.

'What say we offer them a deal, Dad?' said another voice. One of the Macklehose sprigs, of course. So that was the line-up. I pictured it. Three heavies out of condition against two heavies in condition. I'd back the duo, but it could be a damned close-run thing.

'Yes, right, well, what about it, boys?' came the oily Macklehose voice, suddenly tuned for ingratiation. 'There'd be a lot in it for you. Say we split it sixty-forty, eh? I can't say fairer than that, can I?'

'Which way?' said Tingvold, in a voice that suggested mere academic interest.

'Mine, of course.' Macklehose's voice had a self-righteous note in it, and he got very shirty when the two Norwegians laughed unpleasantly. 'I don't think you quite realize that I'm the legal owner of this stuff.'

The Norwegians laughed even louder.

'Why don't you go and see a lawyer, then, Grandad?' said Ratikainen.

'The legal owner is what I am. Miss Carbury, that's the last owner of this stuff, left me all the family items. Says so in the will. She just made a muck-up of the phraseology, silly old cow. I've got my lawyer on to it, don't you worry. Meanwhile, you and me ought to be able to come to a little agreement, eh, boys?'

'Hmmm,' said Ratikainen, the real little sadist. 'I don't know. I think we let the lawyers settle it, don't you, Rolf?'

'Safest thing, Knut,' said Tingvold, playing along. 'Always stick within the law's our motto, right?'

'Aw, come on. You can do a lot better out of this by coming in with me.' In the flickering torchlight I could see Amos Macklehose leaning forward in an agony of evangelical sincerity. 'After all, what are you going to get from this Parfitt guy, eh? A good wage—that's about it, isn't it? Whereas, you throw in your lot with me, and you get part of the sum. I bet you don't know what a thing like that's worth, do you? Look, if I said a million dollars I'd be pitching it low, very low. Think what you could get out of it. What Parfitt's paying you would be peanuts by comparison.'

'Don't give me all this Parfitt this, Parfitt that,' came Rolf Tingvold's voice, with a nasty edge. 'We don't know him. An' I tell you this: if I had to choose between a crooked millionaire and a crooked priest, I choose the millionaire every time.'

I had to hand it to Tingvold. He had his priorities right.

'And I tell you another thing,' Tingvold went on. 'OK, so we do a deal with you, and we pull in the moneys. Very nice. For a time. But what happens then, eh? We don't get no more jobs, that's what happens. Nobody don't trust us no more. Because that's what they know about Knut and me. They give us a job and we do it. Straight along the line, like they say. Sometimes we play it gentle—get results. Sometimes we play it a bit rough—give Knut a bit of fun—get results, just the same. And what they want us to do, we get done, quietly. We get hold of this or that for them, we make somebody disappear, we put the screws on somebody else—all gets done. We fix it. And fix the rap on someone else, if that's how they want it. They hire us because they know we're straight. And we aren't going to do nothing that blows all that—right? We got our reputations to consider.'

He was so respectable he was beginning to sound like a Scandinavian Trade Union leader. At any rate, he seemed to have got through to Macklehose, because when Amos spoke again, his voice was fluttery and unconvincing.

'Now, look, boys. I'm not asking you to break your trust. Would I do that—a man of God? What you've got to remember is that, like I say, I'm the legal owner of this stuff, and—'

But the continued negotiation was all a blind. In mid-sentence he broke off and made a sudden lunge for the manuscript. There was a flailing searchlight of torches as the others realized what he was up to. Then all hell broke loose.

CHAPTER 16

PEREGRINE CONTRA MUNDUM

I guessed at once what he was up to. The idea was that he should grab the manuscript while his young hopefuls kept the heavies busy. In the hysterical confusion of torch beams I saw his hands grab at the large pile of manuscript, while the four others threw themselves towards him and started grappling with each other. It was a real battle of Titans, like something out of Beethoven at his least *gemütlich*. I withdrew into the doorway of the front room, as sounds of grunts, kicks and a shout of anguish suggested that the Scandinavian team was not going to be long in getting the upper hand. As I stood in the darkness of the room, the drab-clad figure of Amos Macklehose emerged running from the study and made along the hall towards the front door.

I delicately put my right foot in his path.

He went crashing forwards towards the foot of the stairs, and there was a terrific bonk as his head made contact with the woodwork. I was meditating going after him and rescuing the manuscript when the sounds of megalithic struggle lessened to a series of whimpers and grunts of concentration. Then, with the sound of a final kick and a groan of pain, one of the thugs came charging out. His torch cast momentary light on the scene. Macklehose was dazedly getting himself up, but was still holding tight to the manuscript with the dogged intensity of a Victorian Methodist clinging to his faith. He saw he could not get to the door and out before he was taken, and with a look of desperation and fear he started, stumbling, up the stairs.

Ratikainen got him before he was halfway up. The frayed carpet tripped him, and Ratikainen threw himself at the scampering legs. The paunchy body of the man of God was stretched upwards towards the bend in the stairs, and the appalling Amos held the manuscript above him and away from his attacker, looking as if he were making an offering to some unwholesome pagan god.

It was a futile gesture. Ratikainen clambered over him, putting in the boot with relish, his torch trained on the bundle of paper. From the doorway of the front room I meditated intervention, but the thought that the odds would turn out to be one against five discouraged me. My main concern was the manuscript, and I flinched as Ratikainen, ending his journey upwards and over the body of Amos Macklehose, arrived at the hands clutching the frail old paper and started tearing it out of Macklehose's grasp. But greed made Amos strong. His grip was frenzied. The Finn put his boot on to Amos's back, heaved and tugged and stamped, but still he couldn't remove it from his grasp. Suddenly there was a horrible rending sound, and I heard the flutter of paper down the stairs.

Any thought I had of emerging and retrieving the pages was stifled by the sound of a howl of pain from the study.

The Macklehose sprigs together had clearly got the upper hand over Rolf Tingvold. The howl had scarcely faded before they were out into the hall and along the stairs. As they trundled up to the aid of their revered pa I saw, horrified, their heavy boots trundling over the pages of the novel that had detached themselves from the bundle. The boys trampled enthusiastically over the two struggling bodies, and while one threw himself at the shoulders of the Finn, the other charged at the disputed manuscript, clutched it in his two hands, and began stamping like a maniac on the wrist of Knut Ratikainen.

But Ratikainen was clearly not the man to be beaten by force of numbers. With a tremendous heave of the body, grunting, but then emitting a strange exultant cry, the Finn heaved off the Macklehose on top of him, and then butted him in the stomach. The boy did a spectacular backwards fall, and only by clutching desperately to the banisters did he stop himself falling head first down the whole flight of stairs. Now Ratikainen turned his attention to the one who was disputing the manuscript, and aimed a karate chop at his neck with his left hand. The blow misfired, but the boy was stopped in his tracks, and howled with pain. Macklehose, though, had wormed his body up into a sitting position, and now got a grip of Ratikainen's leg. It was a pretty sturdy leg, but he now gave it an almighty heave. The three of them collapsed into a mass of flailing limbs, and it was a wonder that any of them heard the voice of Rolf Tingvold, emerging from the study.

'Right. That's it. Any more of that and I shoot.'

He'd been seeing too many old films, that boy. But it worked. Once more there was that comic opera effect of sudden, stunned silence. He came out of the study, and leaned against the doorpost. He had sounded perfectly confident, but in fact he still seemed in pain from a boot placed somewhere vital. The torch in his left hand illuminated the gun in his right, but both of them shook a little. How, even at his best, he could have shot the confused mass of limbs on the stairs and been sure to hit a bit of Macklehose rather than a bit of Ratikainen wasn't quite clear to me, but I thought that perhaps he didn't care. I expect that thought occurred to the people on the stairs too. In any case, one of the Macklehose sprigs was still draped over the banisters, breathing heavily, an obvious target. Above him there was a tangle of limbs that resembled nothing so much as a piece of Hindu artwork. •Amos Macklehose's face was poked out from between a confusion of crotches and ankles, and he was looking at his son. Clearly he was weighing up whether it was worth sacrificing an heir to continue the struggle. Reluctantly he seemed to decide that his chances of keeping the manuscript were small either way. But he kept his hold on.

'Right,' said Rolf Tingvold, with a slight quaver in his voice. 'Now, you three get up, and stand against the wall.'

He came further down the hall, more confidently now, as if the pain was easing. Now, at last, there was a chance for the Bruce Lee stuff. I stood once more in the darkness of the front room, and when the torchlight had gone past me I took a step forward. As he came level with the front room I aimed a lethal kick at the wrist holding the gun.

'Oh Christ!' howled Tingvold, and a clatter told me that my aim had been successful. From the stairs there came the tally-ho of resumed conflict as the whole comic-opera business started up again. By the dim light from the landing I could see that all three Macklehoses were bringing their combined weights to bear on Ratikainen. The grunts were tremendous, and the kicks and the moans — it was all like professional wrestling that was suddenly for real. At the bottom of the stairs Tingvold had got his torch on again, and was scrambling round at the bottom of the coat-stand looking for his gun. He kept looking around him, bewildered, as if to discover how he'd been kicked. Suddenly he spotted his gun and made a grab for it, but the moment he had it in his hand there was a whoop of triumph from the stairs.

'Got it, Dad!' yelled one of the Macklehose young hopefuls, and there was a scampering of feet up the remaining stretch of stairs, on to the level plains of the landing.

The chase was up again. Ratikainen made a grab at the feet of those following the manuscript up to the second floor, but he missed, and, scrambling upright, had to lumber after them. Tingvold was last up, clumping with his Scandinavian boots up the manuscript-strewn stairs. I flinched with pain, and as he gained the top crept out to see the crumpled mess of paper dimly visible in the half light. The two Scandinavians gained the landing together, and as they did so I heard a bolt being slotted triumphantly across: the Macklehoses must have shut themselves into the bathroom.

'Come out of there!' bellowed Tingvold. 'Come on out!'

There was silence. I imagined the Macklehoses inspecting the windows, seeing if the shrubs were climbable.

'Come on out,' Tingvold repeated, 'or I'll shoot the bolt off.'

Standing towards the bottom of the stairs I heard what I took to be some muttered Norwegian. Probably Ratikainen was warning him it would be too noisy (though, heaven knows, they had hardly been behaving like sugar-plum fairies for the last ten minutes). The next thing I heard was the two heavies hurling themselves at the door. It sounded tremendous—like the fall of the temple of Dagon. Once . . . Twice . . .

I slipped back into the front room and switched on the light briefly to locate the telephone.

Three times . . . a great splintering crunch. The door had given way.

I was just about to put my finger on the dial when, through the mayhem that followed, a shot rang out. There was a howl like a rutting wolf which rang through the house, and then total pandemonium reigned upstairs.

I banged down the phone and darted silently up to the landing. In the shadowy half light at the top I looked towards the bathroom. It was brilliantly lighted. Discretion had been cast to the winds, and though the blind had flown up, nobody seemed to care anymore. The whole room was a heaving, grunting mass of bodies,

with one young Macklehose tangling with Knut
Ratikainen over the washbasin, while the other was down
on the floor with Rolf Tingvold, fighting against the
splintered ruins of the door. Between these two tableaux
of agonized, intertwined figures there was one whose
posture was non-combatant and decidedly non-heroic.
Clutching the disintegrating mass of manuscript, now
spluttered with red, was the Reverend Macklehose, sitting
on the bath, and with his other hand glued to his buttock,
from which deep red was flowing into the bathwater. He
had been shot in the bum.

I edged closer to the scene of conflict, unable to
imagine what I could do, but agonized over the fate of the
manuscript. I made it to the door of the nearest bedroom,
and as I did so there was a crash of glass. Ratikainen had
delivered the *coup de grâce* by pushing the head of the
young Macklehose through the window over the basin.
With a grunt of triumph such as saga heroes must have
emitted when they cleaved somebody from the nave to the
chaps he grabbed at the manuscript in the weakening
hand of Amos Macklehose. Amos brought his
bloodstained left hand to bear on the struggle, but victory
was easy. Ratikainen pushed him contemptuously
backwards into the bath and held high the bloody pages.
Then he began a dash for the touchline.

That was his big mistake. The floor of the bathroom
was awash with bathwater, and with a spectacular slide
he landed on top of the spluttering, slithering mass that
was Amos Macklehose. As I watched, almost weeping, I
could see page after page of the manuscript slip out of his
grasp into the reddening water of the bath.

The air was filled with repeated, monotonous
Scandinavian obscenities.

At least the professional thugs were the swifter at
retrieving disaster. Rolf Tingvold directed the sort of
sledge-hammer blow that comic-strip illustrators delight

in at his opponent's chin, and left him dazed and groggy on the floor. He pulled massively at the Finn's arm and hauled him out of the bath. Together they began pulling the sodden, pink, disintegrating pages out of the bathwater. When the Reverend Amos raised his head above the water they pushed him under with gusto, so I suppose they got the fun they had been denied with me.

Me, I was just deciding to tiptoe off downstairs to the phone again when an unfortunate development occurred. The young Macklehose who had had his head pushed through the window had now scrambled back and, sobbing and groaning, was dabbing his handkerchief over a great gash that extended from his forehead to his chin. He sank down from his position sprawled over the basin to sit weeping noisily on the loo. Ratikainen looked at him, as if meditating further violence. But before he could decide which of the jolly japes in his madly amusing repertoire to employ, a thought forced its way painfully through his thick skull.

'Where's the cop?'

There was silence. Even the sobbing stopped.

'What did you say?' said Tingvold.

'Where's the cop? We left him here.'

'What cop?' gurgled Macklehose, scrambling upright in the bath and looking very little like Venus rising from the waves.

'That cop — the big one — that's been on this thing. We left him here. Tied up.'

'Someone tripped me, down in the hall,' gargled Macklehose.

'Someone kicked the gun out of my hand,' said Tingvold. 'The bugger's escaped.'

I withdrew into the depths of the bedroom as they stood there, looking at each other.

'Grab what you can,' I heard Ratikainen yell.

From the window of the bedroom I caught sight

suddenly of a dark shape behind a privet hedge. Then another. Then I saw a helmet. And some way down the road I saw what I was sure was a police car, its identifying lights turned off. Someone must have phoned. The cavalry had arrived!

'Right. I'm getting out of here,' shouted Rolf Tingvold from the bathroom. Definitely too many gangster films, that boy.

He was the first past me, along the landing, clutching a great unwieldy mass of dripping manuscript. He was followed by Ratikainen, similarly burdened, dripping pools of water and casting backwards longing, vengeful looks at the other three. The Macklehose boys bore only a page or two each, snatched in flight. And bringing up the rear, and clutching his bum, came the Reverend Macklehose, squelching and sobbing, and hugging the little bunch of pages he had managed to retain. He flopped downstairs like a suction rubber on a wet draining-board, and was the last out through the front door of No. 45, Jubilee Parade.

Oh, the joy of standing in that darkened window and watching them as, one after another, they hared down the front path into the arms of the waiting police!

CHAPTER 17

ONE FELL SWOOP

And a pretty spectacle we all made! As I came down the path to the little front gate I paused to survey them in the light of the street-lamp. Amos Macklehose so sodden and bloody that he had made a whole pink pool on the dry summer pavement. One of his sons blue with bruises, and with a tooth missing; the other with a great gash down the side of his face and blood dripping down on to his shirt. Rolf Tingvold was comparatively unscathed, but Knut Ratikainen was soaking and battered, though in the lamplight his wet face still contrived to look impassively menacing.

And there was me, my shirt bloodsoaked and torn from neck to waist, and a bloody hand-towel stuffed into the waist of my trousers. As I came out of the gate one of the constables came out with handcuffs and made to arrest me. I really could see his point. Luckily the inspector in charge was one of the men I'd talked to at the West Yorkshire Metropolitan Police HQ. In spite of everything he recognized me.

'Real little Falklands conflict in there,' he said.

'Have you got the manuscript?' I asked.

'Manuscript? Was that the paper they were all clutching? Oh yes — that constable over there's got it.'

I went over to a police van, where a young constable was throwing the dripping sheets any old how into the back.

'Here, give that to me,' I said. 'It's valuable.'

'Could have fooled me,' said the constable, looking at the sticky mess with scepticism.

'Could be worth a million,' I said, accepting Amos Macklehose's valuation. Who better to put a price on things than a Californian man of God? I took the miserable bundle in my arms and went back to talk to the inspector.

'You look like you need a trip to the field hospital,' he said, in that nice, flat, Yorkshire way.

'I came lightly off the field of battle,' I said. 'In comparison with this lot, anyway.'

I went to the pool of light and looked them over. They stood in a row, shivering, handcuffed. Amos was still sobbing — great, gurgly sobs that suggested he still had a lot of bathwater inside him. The son with the great gash was snivelling too, and to be fair he had good cause. Rolf Tingvold looked straight ahead, as if he were on guard duty. But Knut Ratikainen looked me in the face, unflinching, until suddenly he narrowed his eyes and spat—a fast, vicious and accurate gob.

On top of it all it didn't seem to matter. I didn't even bother to wipe it off.

'Nice lot,' said the inspector. 'Especially that one. I don't know if you saw but he gave one of my boys a nasty injury when we took him in. Kicked like a stallion.'

'Assaulting a police officer,' I said. 'One more charge. Not that we'll need charges with that one. This—' I pointed to my belly—'comes under a similar heading, though I can think of a lot nastier words than assault that would fit it. Anyway, we'll be preparing a whole string of charges for this little lot as a whole—it'll keep your men down at HQ tap-tapping away at their typewriters for hours.'

'Good,' said the inspector. 'They look like the kind that ought to be put away for some time. What do we begin with?'

'Oh, burglary, intimidation, grievous bodily harm—that kind of thing. By the way, I'm afraid Leeds will be losing one of its churches.'

'I beg your pardon, sir?'

'This gentleman is pastor, or leader, or something, of the Tabernacle of the Risen Moses.'

'Can't say I know the show. Not part of the Established Church, I suppose.'

'I certainly hope not, but anyway he's a pastor, and I can't see his wife carrying on the good work.'

'It doesn't sound like a body-blow to the religious life of the community, I must say, sir. Funny, it's usually a quite different sort of charge we get clerical gentlemen on.'

'Well now, these three are all the one family, and you can charge them with breaking and entering for a start.

They broke and entered this house tonight, and I'm a witness to it. Keep them at the station tonight and I'll give them a good going-over in the morning.'

'I'm sure you'll enjoy that. And these other chappies—German, are they?'

'Norwegians. The Viking spirit turned nasty. Do you remember they had that Exhibition a few years ago, and kept going on about how the Vikings were really only peaceable farmers and traders?'

'Now you mention it, I did see something about them on TV.'

'Well, I'll need a lot of convincing about that after my dealings with this little lot. You can do the GBH routine with them—again, just for a start. You'll have my evidence, for one. I'll get a doctor to look at this little minor operation they did on me, and get him to send you a report. I should think, now, we might be able to get something out of Tetterfield.'

'Who, sir?'

'Tetterfield. A stark raving librarian in a profession that tends towards the drab. If it hadn't been for Tetter-field—'

You know, that was one time in my career when real life did things on cue. The name was no sooner out of my mouth than, rounding the corner from Cardigan Road into the Parade, and coming immediately under the flood of street-light there, there appeared the figures of Tetterfield and Timothy Scott-Windlesham. Walking tentatively, with almost exaggerated caution, they advanced a few steps. A reconnoitring expedition, by God! Perhaps another little amateur break-in! They advanced, stopped, and gaped into the circus of police activity in the Parade. Tetterfield was slow. He squinted into the lights as if he had suddenly found himself in a television studio. Timothy rapped out some words, and then did an abrupt full turn and started back to the main road.

'Get them!' I shouted to two of the constables. They stood for a moment, astonished, and I shouted again: 'Get them!' and started after them myself.

But after a few steps I left it to the constables. They were much younger and lighter, and didn't have gaping wounds in their bellies. Mine had opened up again, and I had to sit down on the bonnet of the police car, clutching my pain.

It wasn't much of a chase. Tetterfield was hardly in condition to keep his lead over the young policeman, and he gave up without a struggle. Timothy was faster, but the constable got him just as he was hailing a passing taxi fifty yards down Cardigan Road. When the two of them got back Timothy was in a great wax of grievance, but the constable was grinning like a Cheshire cat. He obviously hadn't enjoyed an arrest so much since joining the force.

'Will you tell this young oaf to release me, and tell me what you think you're doing?' piped Timothy in his high-pitched whine, addressing the inspector. 'I've been manhandled by him while going about my perfectly lawful business. If things go on like this, we'll be like America, unable to walk the streets at night. Will you tell me what you think all this is in aid of?'

'Perhaps you'll tell me first why you started to run,' suggested the inspector, who had a very good line in impassivity.

'Run? Is it a crime to jog? I run for my health.'

'You looked more to me as if you were running for your life. And you're not really dressed for jogging, are you, sir? Well, we'll go into that down at the station.'

'The station? This is ridiculous! You haven't a thing to charge me with. What am I supposed to have done?'

'What you are supposed to have done,' I said, getting up from the bonnet of the car, 'is attack Miss Edith Wing in her cottage on the evening of June the eighth.' He saw me for the first time, recognized me, and cringed a little. 'And I'm going to see that we charge you, and make the charge stick. And if this gentleman here—' I turned to Tetterfield—'isn't more co-operative than he's been so far, he'll find himself up as an accessory before and after the fact, and sent down for a very long period. *That* I can promise him. *Not* a very peaceful way to spend your twilight years.'

They were bundled into the police car, Timothy blustering, but without conviction, Tetterfield thoughtful.

'What a horrible little twerp,' said the constable who had taken Timothy. 'But the other one didn't look like a crook.'

'A silly man,' I said. 'For all I know certifiable. But I hope not.'

'He'll talk,' said the inspector. He and the constable and I were now standing by the gate of No. 45. The constable nodded his agreement.

'Looked like it,' I said. 'I certainly hope so. When he hears the manuscript is safe in some bank vault or other, what's left of it, he'll probably come clean as a whistle, given the right sort of inducement.'

'Is it important?' asked the inspector.

'Vital, if we're going to nail that feeble twit who attacked Miss Wing. I doubt we'll get much other evidence. It'll be useful with the two Scands too—help to get them on a double charge, and bring a really nasty sentence down on them, given the right judge.'

'All your chicks in one fell swoop,' said the young constable. Then he blushed, and muttered: 'Did it for "O" level.'

'I only wish it were true,' I said. 'I shouldn't be ungrateful—it's one hell of a haul of villains. But there's one golden chick, the biggest of the brood, and him I haven't got.'

'Who's that, then?'

'The man behind the whole thing—or at least behind the two Scands. An American millionaire called Parfitt.'

The inspector shook his head dubiously.

'Funny, isn't it, how the biggest fishes always slip through the net.'

'I netted some once,' I said reminiscently. 'But not this time. He'll be out swimming in the big ocean by now, I'm afraid. Those two Scands would have to talk, for us to get him now.'

'And they won't?'

'No. Not if they run true to form. They behave as if they've taken some kind of thugs' Masonic oath. Anyway, I'll be sending a nice little report on our suspicions to the FBI. It's something. Mr James L. Parfitt won't have quite such a lily-white record in the future.'

'It's not the same, though,' said the constable.

'Not the same at all. In this job you have to settle for second best most of the time, and think yourself lucky. Ah well, I'd better go back in.'

'Into the house?' said the inspector. 'What for?'

'Clean up,' I said laconically.

'Do you want a guard on the house?'

'No. I'll be here all night. That'll be enough. I might manage a couple of hours' kip on the sofa, if I'm lucky. Could you send someone for me early in the morning? Then we can have a good session going over these villains.'

'Will do.'

So I went, almost reluctantly, back up the front path to the door. Behind me, the police began packing things up, and driving away. The neighbours, I imagine, started disappearing behind their unlighted windows to prepare themselves milky nightcaps, resolved to find out in the morning what it had all been about. Steeling myself, I opened the front door and turned on the hall light. It was a grisly sight. Paper, sodden and trampled, was strewn all the way down the stairs. A great trail of water stretched from the landing down to the door, mingled with blood from the Macklehose buttocks. There was a musty smell to the house, probably its habitual odour, and I left the door ajar. This looked like an all-night job. I dumped the bundle of manuscript retrieved from the villains on the floor and crept gingerly round the trampled sheets on the stairs, up to the bathroom.

What a scene of blood and desolation! The mess was indescribable, and somehow unreal, like the set for a Dracula film. There in the pink waters of the bath were three pages, floating forlornly. I retrieved them cautiously. They were so saturated that the writing had all but disappeared. In the great wash on the floor I picked out a further wad of sheets—nearly as wet, and clinging together. Under the basin was a single, limp leaf.

I took them out to the landing. Then I went into the bedrooms, switched the lights on, and laid the separate sheets out over the bedroom carpet, cautiously separating those in the sodden bundle. I wasn't sure I was doing the right thing, but when I surveyed the scene I felt pleased with myself.

Then I went down the stairs, taking up the damp, torn, crumpled and boot-dirtied sheets and laying them out carefully, a few on each stair. They were hideously damaged, but not, I thought, irretrievably. Then I got to the large bundle I'd placed in the hall, pulled from the fat, greedy fingers of Amos Macklehose, and the leaner fingers of the Scands. I put the lights on in the study and the front room—the house had probably not been so well lit since its great Edwardian days—and started separating the sheets, blowing dust and dirt off the dry ones, laying the wet ones out carefully. It was quite quiet outside, and I sat, cross-legged, on the hall floor, suddenly feeling oddly happy.

'Perry!'

I jumped a foot, and swung round to the front door.

'Jan! How in hell—'

'Oh God, Perry—look!'

I looked down at my gory shirt and the bloodsoaked towel.

'Oh, it's not as serious as it looks.'

'Not you. The manuscript. Oh God—it's ruined.'

'Some of it. I think we can save a fair bit. Jan, if you want to be useful, sit down and help dry these out. What the hell are you doing here, anyway?'

'I got worried. When you said you were going in. Well, you *were* a fathead, Perry, to do it on your own. You needn't expect me to sympathize with your wounds. So I left Daniel in charge of Aunt Kate, and got in the car.'

'Really, Jan. Do you think I can't take care of myself?'

'Yes, I do. Obviously you can't. Anyway, when I finally found the place, all hell was loose in the house. I was terrified—it was like there was a herd of elephants penned up in here. So I went to the phone-box and diailed the police.'

'Oh Christ, Jan! You didn't! What's it going to look like? The great man from Scotland Yard with the little wifey who follows him round to make sure he doesn't get hurt.'

'I didn't give my name,' said Jan demurely. 'I was tender of your bloody *amour propre*. I said it was a neighbour. Though all the real neighbours were glued in front of the late-night movie, and I don't think they noticed a thing until all the police started arriving.'

'Well—' I said, mollified. 'That was bright of you.'

'Don't condescend,' said Jan. 'You should be bloody grateful to me. I've had a good case. Whereas you, Perry . . .'

'Don't rub it in. I've had my good cases.'

'This wasn't one of them.'

'I suffered in the cause,' I said, nodding down to my midriff.

'What is it? Obviously not a bullet.'

'The Finn put his knife in. And twisted it.'

'Hmmm. No woman who's had a baby is going to be very impressed by *that*.'

'Thanks very much. You're having a dampening effect on me, Jan. I was feeling good before you came.'

'Well, you may think you've done a fabulous job, but I don't. I mean, you came up here to get the manuscript back—'

'Well—and didn't I?'

'But in what sort of condition? And the fact is, if I hadn't rung the police, the whole lot of them would have got away, and the whole thing would have been practically scattered to the four winds.'

We laid out the last two pages, and stood up and surveyed our work.

'Oh, Perry, it's awful! It makes me weep. OK—it's probably all there—but look at it!'

'I don't know. Scientists can work wonders these days.'

'Well, they can't work miracles. Some of it's obviously gone forever. It was difficult enough to decipher before, and no whatsitoscope is going to get it back now. That's what's so terrible. There's going to be this great book, with big gaps where they have to say that the manuscript is indecipherable. It'll be like the Elgin Marbles—all chipped about, and bits fallen off.'

'I don't think so,' I said.

'You're just being stupidly optimistic.'

'Come through here,' I said, leading her into the back room. I pointed to the desk.

'See those piles. Macklehose grabbed the biggest pile when he started the whole fracas. That's what's out there. That's the bit that's already been transcribed. Here's Miss

Boothroyd's typescript. This small pile is the rest of it. She must have been working on the top page of this when I came calling. See — there's still a page half-finished in the machine. If Emily Brontë finished the novel, then we'll have all of it.'

Jan looked at it, and swallowed. Her spirits, always a bit mercurial, rose, and she looked at me and smiled. Then she went towards the piles on the desk.

'Oh, Perry — it's incredible. Then this is *it*.' She took up the typescript. 'This is the novel no one living has read.'

'Except Miss Boothroyd.'

'I don't begrudge it her. She doesn't sound as if she's had much fun. Look at it. She's done a marvellous job.'

We peered together at the typescript. Jan sat down in the desk chair, and I swung one over from the table. We put on the desk light and gazed at the neatly typed first page.

That summer, the summer of my twenty-second year, was the last summer of my content. July and August had been hot, with blazing sun and heavy air, presaging storms that never came. The only breeze vouchsafed us fluttered listlessly over the moors, and I ranged them, gun in hand, at peace with myself and all else, except the creatures of nature that I coveted for my supper. It was in that frame of mind, one day in the first week of September, that I climbed to the top of Mendith Crag, to gaze down on the drear, blank-windowed spectacle of Lingdale Manor.

I stopped short, and clung to the solitary stripling ash that braved the winds of the crag. The windows were curtained, the chimneys were smoking. Three carts, loaded with furniture, stood in the yard, and the farm cats that had used to dispute the tenancy with each other were now scrutinizing angrily the human intruders.

The Thornleys had returned, as my father had always predicted.

Indeed, as I watched, there came round the corner from the ruined kitchen garden, a young woman, drably dressed in grey cotton, but so striking of face and bearing that I clung more tightly to the stripling ash. This was my first glimpse of Marian Thornley.

We settled down to a long night's reading.

Robert B. PARKER

"The toughest, funniest, wisest private-eye in the field."*

☐ A CATSKILL EAGLE	....	11132-3	$3.95
☐ CEREMONY	....	10993-0	$4.50
☐ EARLY AUTUMN	....	12214-7	$4.50
☐ GOD SAVE THE CHILD	....	12899-4	$4.50
☐ THE GODWULF MANUSCRIPT	....	12961-3	$4.50
☐ THE JUDAS GOAT	....	14196-6	$4.50
☐ LOOKING FOR RACHEL WALLACE	....	15316-6	$3.95
☐ LOVE AND GLORY	....	14629-1	$4.50
☐ MORTAL STAKES	....	15758-7	$4.50
☐ PALE KINGS AND PRINCES	....	20004-0	$4.50
☐ PROMISED LAND	....	17197-0	$3.95
☐ A SAVAGE PLACE	....	18095-3	$4.50
☐ TAMING A SEA-HORSE	....	18841-5	$4.50
☐ VALEDICTION	....	19246-3	$4.50
☐ THE WIDENING GYRE	....	19535-7	$4.50
☐ WILDERNESS	....	19328-1	$4.50

*The Houston Post